KW-241-957

FIRING SQUAD

"Don't I get one last smoke?" Gatling asked.

"As you wish," the lieutenant said. Some of the soldiers were talking and the lieutenant turned to shout at them.

Gatling pulled the stick of Maximite from under his collar and touched off the one-inch fuse, grabbing the lieutenant's holstered .44 at the same time. He shot the sergeant first because he had a rifle. The lieutenant was no coward and he shouted, "Open fire, open fire!" Gatling shot him in the heart as he tried to grab the gun. Loading levers were clacking. Gatling threw the smoking stick of Maximite at the firing squad, and then ducked behind the post. The stick was light and it fell short, but after it exploded there was nothing left but mangled bodies and a hole in the ground . . . .

Also in the GATLING series:

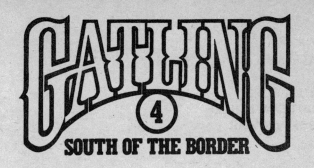

GATLING

4

SOUTH OF THE BORDER

JACK SLADE

LEISURE BOOKS   **NEW YORK CITY**

A LEISURE BOOK®

September 1989

Published by

Dorchester Publishing Co., Inc.
276 Fifth Avenue
New York, NY 10001

Copyright©1989 by Dorchester Publishing Co., Inc.

All rights reserved. No part of this book may be reproduced or transmitted in any form by any electronic or mechanical means, including photocopying, recording, or by any information storage and retrieval system, without the written permission of the Publisher, except where permitted by law.

The name "Leisure Books" and the stylized "LB" with design are trademarks of Dorchester Publishing Co., Inc.

Printed in the United States of America.

Prologue

The rebel lieutenant's watch was fast or he was in a hurry. It wasn't sunrise yet, but he came to the adobe house where Gatling was under heavy guard and told him it was time to be shot. The lieutenant looked as if he'd been a clerk or a village schoolteacher before he joined the National Independence Army of Panama. He wore eyeglasses and a mustache and a neatly patched uniform: the kind of man who liked to shuffle and reshuffle papers. He had fooled with papers during Gatling's trial, over which he'd presided in the absence of higher authority. He'd delivered a number of speeches in the course of which he'd denounced Yankee imperialism and extolled the magnificent qualities of the Panamanian People. The villagers, who'd been forced to witness the trial, had stood silent and uncomprehending until prodded into vigorous applause by the bayonets of the lieutenant's soldiers.

Worn out by his own oratory, the lieutenant had found Gatling guilty and sentenced him to be shot at sunrise of the following day. Now, attended by a sergeant with his stripes painted on the sleeves of his ragged shirt, the lieutenant read the order of execution in flowery Spanish before he repeated it in a few words of plain English.

"You see we observe the formalities," he stated. "You have

been sentenced to be shot at sunrise, and that is what we do."
The lieutenant drew himself up to his full height of five feet,
two inches. "Please not to make any trouble. No priest will
be permitted. We are anticlerical: All the priests have been
shot." The lieutenant patted the plain rubber grip of his
Remington .44. "I shot the priest who baptized me. It was the
least I could do to wash away the stain of his witchcraft."

Good for you, Gatling thought. Maybe I can return the favor.
The true believers were the worst, the revolutionaries who didn't
steal. At his so-called trial, he'd tried to explain that he had
come to Panama as a member of an American expedition whose
sole purpose was to find the best route for a canal across the
Isthmus. The United States had no dark designs on Panamanian
territory, he'd said. The expedition had received permission for
its work from the Colombian government and the Governor of
Panama, Tomas Suarez de Cordoba.

That had been a mistake, not that anything he said would have
made any difference. The lieutenant had shouted him down.
"Tyrants! Traitors!" he'd shouted. "The Panamanian People
need bread, not canals. Canals for your Yankee battleships!
Let the Yankees dig that trench. We will bury them in it."

Now they were marching him out past the end of the village
where a tree trunk had been cut down to six feet. Years before,
the bark had been stripped and iron fetters driven into the wood.
The execution post was pocked and splintered with the bullets
of many executions, and the ground around it had been cleared
and trampled flat. Behind it the jungle, dark and green, came
in close. Birds and monkeys were squawking and chattering in
the trees. It wasn't quite sunrise, but it was steaming hot. Except
for the mountains, it was always hot in Panama.

There was even a crudely made coffin for him to be buried
in: The prissy lieutenant was observing all the formalities.
Usually they dumped you in a shallow grave, and that night
the dogs dug you up for a moonlight feast. Gatling figured he
wouldn't need the coffin if the stick of Maximite worked the
way it was supposed to. Maximite, the latest invention of
Hudson Maxim, brother of the weapons king Hiram Maxim,

was 50 percent more powerful than dynamite. The slender stick of Maximite, now tucked inside his shirt collar, was equal to one standard stick of dynamite. The trouble was, they had broken it when they searched his boots. They had found the knife in the lining of his boot, but missed the Maximite. But broken though it was, the fiber that ran through it held it together. It looked like a very thin candle snapped in several places and still joined by the wick. Even if they hadn't taken his match case, he could not have used it to blow out the wall of the makeshift jail. It was too powerful; he would have been blown to stew meat. And now, getting closer to the execution post, he still didn't have a match.

Barefoot villagers watched from the edge of the execution ground. That was the law; they had to be there. If they had any interest in the proceedings, it was because this time the condemned man was an American. No one in Panama liked Americans, but to put one in front of a firing squad was most unusual. In color, the villagers ranged from shoe-polish black to jaundice yellow. They looked with longing at Gatling's clothes and boots, but knew the soldiers had first crack.

The firing squad took up their positions. The sergeant followed Gatling and the lieutenant to the execution post. Only seven men were billeted in the village: the lieutenant, the sergeant, the five soldiers. Not so bad, Gatling thought. He didn't think the villagers would want to mix in. Revolutions came and went, and they still ate fried monkey meat and bananas. They might be glad to bury the lieutenant and his men.

The execution post was stained with the blood of the enemies of this latest revolution and all the others that had gone before it. After adjusting his eyeglasses, the lieutenant took a folded paper from his pocket, and the sergeant stepped forward to manacle Gatling's wrists and ankles.

"Don't I get one last smoke?" Gatling asked before the sergeant could touch him. "A last request . . . a civilized man like you . . . ."

"As you wish," the lieutenant said. He liked to be thought of as civilized. He was so pleased he reminded Gatling of a monkey pissing on Sunday visitors through the bars of his cage. He took a thin cigar from the shirt pocket and Gatling stuck it in his mouth. The lieutenant lit it with a match he struck on the execution post.

"Ah," Gatling said, sucking in smoke to make the tip of the cigar burn bright.

"You don't have to smoke all of it," the lieutenant said impatiently. Gatling knew the lieutenant intended to smoke the rest of the cigar after the execution was carried out. Some of the soldiers were talking and the lieutenant turned to shout at them.

"*Silencio!*" he shouted. "*Quieto!*"

Gatling pulled the stick of Maximite from under his collar and touched off the one-inch fuse, grabbing the lieutenant's holstered .44 at the same time. He shot the sergeant first because he had a rifle. The lieutenant was no coward and he shouted, "Open fire, open fire!" Gatling shot him in the heart as he tried to grab the gun. Loading levers were clacking. Gatling threw the smoking stick of Maximite at the firing squad, and then ducked behind the post. The stick was light and it fell short, but after it exploded there was nothing left but mangled bodies and a hole in the ground.

For an instant the villagers were paralyzed by their own astonishment, caught like figures in a posed photograph, and then they were gone.

Gatling ran for the jungle . . . .

Chapter
ONE

"Why don't they build the canal across Nicaragua?" Gatling asked. "It's flatter, has a better climate, a better government, two big lakes that could be joined."

Colonel Pritchett lay back in his chair and puffed on his pipe. They were in the colonel's office in the Maxim Company's warehouse on Crosby Street in New York City. Gatling worked for the Maxim Company, testing its latest weapons under combat conditions.

"Thank you, Professor Gatling," the colonel said. "I wasn't aware that you held an engineering degree. But for now the Isthmus of Panama is what it has to be. Yes, I know. DeLesseps has been trying to build a Panama canal for years. Without much to show for it, I might add. Thus far he's managed to kill twenty thousand workmen, and his company is bankrupt and under investigation for fraud. Bilking the investors, and so on. Now the United States wants to take a crack at it. Good old Britain doesn't like that, but there isn't a hell of a lot they can do about it."

"Then it's been decided," Gatling said.

"Good Lord, no," the colonel said. "Washington never decides anything in haste. The wheels of government are oblong instead of round, producing a sort of stop-and-go motion. But if there is finally a firm decision, my spies tell me it will be Panama. Actually, there are a number of things that make Panama the ideal place for a canal. The Isthmus, at its narrowest point, is only fifty miles wide, and it isn't quite as threatened by volcanoes and earthquakes as Nicaragua is. While it's true that the climate—''

''The climate is about the worst in the world,'' Gatling said, cutting in. ''It rains and steams and stinks. Down there they have yellow fever, malaria, cholera, dengue, galloping consumption. You can take quinine for malaria, but what can you do about yellow fever and cholera?''

''Die, I suppose,'' the colonel said.

''They don't call it the white man's graveyard for nothing. The mosquitoes and sand flies drive you crazy. In the swamps, along the rivers, they got crocodiles—I'm not talking about alligators—that'll come right into camp looking for a meal. I've been there, Colonel.''

''I keep forgetting that,'' the colonel said. ''How long was it?''

''A couple of weeks,'' Gatling said. ''I don't claim to know the country, but I know what I saw.''

''What were you doing there in the first place?'' the colonel asked, as if he didn't know. ''Oh, yes, I remember now. You delivered some Gatling guns to some rebel group, but they didn't want to pay. You had to kill rather a lot of the poor fellows before their leader came down from the hills and apologized for the misunderstanding. He paid in full, but chased you through the swamps trying to get his money back. Must have been quite exciting.''

Gatling ignored all that. Colonel Harry Pritchett was a genuine son of a bitch, always trying to get the advantage of the other man. Since he'd been kicked out of the British Army for slaughtering two hundred Afghan prisoners—his only son was tortured and killed during the second Afghan War—he'd loved nothing and no one. There were times when Gatling liked the colonel well enough, and there were times when he would gladly have strangled the sarcastic, overbearing bastard. But feelings didn't have much to do with it; they could do business together, and had.

The colonel contitnued. "Everything you've said about Panama has been said before, all of it bad. Columbia owns the province but can't control it. We will take it over when the time is right, but we won't need to go into that. Let's leave politics to the politicians. What we're concerned with is finding the right place to dig. Murdock Wheeler will lead the expedition. You know the name?"

Gatling said he did. Everybody who read the newspaper knew who Murdock Wheeler was. A builder of railroads, bridges, and tunnels, he was famous all over the world. At 40, flamboyant and self-serving, he was known as the friend of kings and presidents, and although he was sometimes accused of taking credit for other men's work, he had the reputation of getting things done. Not the least of his accomplishments was his ability to raise huge sums of money.

"How big is this expedition?" Gatling asked.

"Fifty people so far," the colonel said. "Surveyors, draftsmen, geologists, engineers. Don't ask me to sort them out. Two doctors, a photographer and his assistant, one or two newspapermen. Wheeler will be taking along his own cook. All you lesser mortals will have the other cook."

Gatling wasn't interested in cooks. "How many soldiers—Marines—whatever they are?"

"Marines. It's a Navy show," the colonel said. "Twenty marines. Two lieutenants, eighteen enlisted men. Yes, yes. I realize that's not nearly enough. Before you start getting hot under the collar, let me point out that no soldiers of any kind will be accompanying this expedition. Officially, that is. Wheeler and Washington had to agree to that or the Colombian government would not have given its permission. These men will not be in uniform, but will be listed on the payroll as laborers."

"What's the reason for all this?" Gatling asked. "The first expedition had more than fifty uniformed regulars armed with rifles."

"Quite correct," the colonel said. "But that was eighteen years ago and times—and governments—change. This is 1888, and the United States is fast becoming a global sea power, which is the principal reason for wanting a canal which will join the two oceans. The government of Columbia may be made up of thieving half-castes, but they aren't completely stupid. They don't want Uncle Sam to turn into a tyrannical father. In short, they smell a rat."

The colonel liked to hear himself talk.

"Why didn't they just say no?"

"Money talks," the colonel said. "Wheeler's go-between had to cross a few greasy palms with silver. Gold, actually. They like gold. Permission was granted but only if certain conditions were agreed to. One of them was: no soldiers in or out of uniform. We're breaking our word, of course, but they won't mind as long as we're not too flagrant about it."

"How do I fit into this? The Maxim Company?" Whatever it was, Gatling knew it wouldn't be on the up and up. But he wasn't complaining; the weapons business was always a bit shady.

The colonel adjusted his black eyepatch. It gave him one more thing to fool with. He was a man of mannerisms. He filled his foul-smelling pipe like a surgeon preparing to operate. He tugged at his nicotine-stained mustache. And in the last year or so, since he'd lost an eye helping Gatling to fight the Zuni-Apache war in New Mexico, he'd had the eyepatch to fiddle with. He could have afforded the best, most natural-looking glass eye in New York, but he preferred the eyepatch.

"Where do you come in?" the colonel said. "Where you always do. With the automatic weapons, the heavy hardware —and there is the Maxim Company's newest invention, an explosive called Maximite. In point of fact, it was invented by Mr. Maxim's brother, Hudson, but we'll discuss it later. For now, let me assure you that it's fifty percent more powerful than dynamite."

"You're expecting trouble?"

"That's putting it mildly," the colonel said. "We must face facts, old man. Some of those Marines are going to die. Microbes, germs, the little beasties that wriggle under the microscope are going to get them. In Panama, the death rate for foreigners is one in three. Some of the civilians will die too, but at the moment that's not our concern. Our concern is to give this expedition a fighting chance. That means you. You are to be the heavy gun."

"What if the little beasties lay me low?"

The colonel's laugh sounded like a rusty hinge. "Come now, you old blackguard, you know you're too mean to be killed by a microbe. If a fer-de-lance bites you, the snake will die. One look at you and a hungry crocodile will run for bicarbonate of soda."

"You should join a tent show," Gatling said. "You could sit on the Fat Lady's knee and tell jokes. I asked you where the Maxim Company comes into this. It can't be peddling guns. Is Maxim doing it as a favor to Wheeler? The Navy Department?"

"As a *dis*favor to Commodore Vanderbilt's Panama Railway," the colonel said. "Mr. Maxim wouldn't share a cup of water with Wheeler in the middle of the Sahara. Thinks him a cad. So do I, if it matters. It all boils down to this: When Mr. Maxim had his first great success with the Maxim .303, he invited the Commodore to some bally great bash he was throwing at his country house in Surrey. The Commodore was in Britain at the time. One captain of industry to another. Except that the Commodore didn't acknowledge the invitation, and didn't show up. Not only that, the Commodore had some rather nasty things he said about Mr. Maxim. I think he referred to Mr. Maxim as 'this rustic mechanic.' "

"Then it's just spite," Gatling said.

"Not entirely. This canal will be the greatest engineering feat since the pyramids and the Brooklyn Bridge. Much more important than the Suez, I think, and much more profitable. The Panama Railway was fine in its day, and still serves a useful purpose, but after all, you can't put a battleship on a flatcar.

But there's no money in battleships except for those who build them. Mr. Maxim owns fifty-one percent of the shipping line. He has a financial interest, yes. Needless to say, the railway johnnies don't want a canal.''

"How much don't they want it?''

"Their agents are already hiring gunmen. In this country and in Panama. And not just down-and-outers who fancy themselves as mercenaries. They're hiring the best—the worst—men they can find, and they're paying top wages. A man named William Frobisher—hates to be called Billy—will lead them, and believe me, he knows how to do it. Ever hear of him?''

Gatling said yes. "Used to be a Regular Army captain before he was kicked out for extreme cruelty to his men. Must have been pretty cruel to get dumped from the frontier army. Later he turned up as a strikebreaker for some detective agency. Killed a lot of miners in Colorado. Last I heard of him he was gunrunning in Central America.''

"Right now he's in New Orleans, or was. That's the jumping-off place for his little army. The Panama Railway is backing him all the way. Money no object. The Morgan Bank is one of the principal villains. There are others, but J.P. himself is stage center. Nothing that can be proved, naturally, but Morgan and his henchmen are dead set against this expedition.''

"You said that two or three times, Colonel. What else? Can we appeal to the provincial governor if it gets very bad?''

'' 'Fraid not,'' the colonel answered. "You see, the Colombians have taken money from both sides. Which is their idea of being fair. Governor Suarez wants to set himself up as president of a new Panamanian republic, so he's playing it very close to the vest. The Colombians don't trust him, but he isn't an easy man to get rid of. He has the backing of the Provincial Guard, as they call it, and other rich Colombians resident in Panama see him as a way to hog the entire trough. And there are the rebels of the National Independence Army, Urbino's dirty-shirt brigade. Call himself El Tigre, and he keeps on nipping at the Governor's heels.''

"Sounds great,'' Gatling said. "A walk in the woods, except

some son of a bitch will be sniping at us from behind every tree. Any chance of buying off this Urbino? These rebel swamp-trotters are always hurting for money.''

"A waste of money," the colonel said. "DeLesseps tried to buy him with money and guns and just made it worse. He used the guns against the French and used the money to buy more guns. Urbino didn't like the French, but he absolutely hates Americans. Years ago some American called him a dirty nigger and he hasn't forgotten. Of course he is some kind of nigger—aren't they all—but it was the way it was said. His mammy and pappy came from Trinidad, and they spoke island English, and so does he, and never mind the El Tigre nonsense. That's just window dressing for the spicks. They spick Spanish, so El Tigre he is."

The colonel took a map case from the deep drawer of his blond-oak desk and rolled out a map of Panama. He anchored the map with two paperweights, a silver letter-opener, and a small artillery shell. He brushed up the ends of his military mustache, and his good eye gleamed.

"Gather round, gentlemen," he snapped, thinking of better, bloodier times.

Maybe the old shit was getting senile, Gatling thought, as he gathered round. The colonel used a steel-nibbed pen as a pointer. "The expedition will land at San Blas Bay," he said in a schoolteacher voice. "Otherwise known as the Bay of Mosquitoes."

Gatling looked where the colonel was pointing. "Why not Limon Bay? That's where the first expedition came ashore."

"Good Christ! Must you keep interrupting? Limon Bay is the best place to land, but it's too obvious."

"Obvious! What the hell are you talking about? It looks like the opposition knows as much about this expedition as Wheeler does. So why wouldn't they know where it's going to land?"

The colonel stabbed the Bay of Mosquitoes with the steel pen. "Blast you!" he said. "Will you leave the planning to the planners. This . . . this fucking place is where they—you—are going to land. It's been decided by better minds than yours."

Gatling said, "Into the valley of death rode the six hundred. Who wrote that? James Whitcomb Riley?" Gatling pulled the pen out of the map. "Here's your pointer, sir."

The colonel simmered down. His fits of temper never lasted long. After years of shouting at subordinates, he could turn it off and on. He knew he needed Gatling. So did Gatling.

"Let's agree that it's a dunderheaded idea," he said. "But it's been decided, it's set in concrete, nothing *we* can do to change it, eh?"

Gatling liked that *we* bullshit. Whenever the colonel wanted to get close on the dance floor, he used the word *we*, as if they were equals, the best of friends.

"From the Bay of Mosquitoes the expedition will proceed inland. What an adventure, eh? If only I could go with you." Gatling figured the colonel would be dining at Delmonico's while he was trying to dodge poisoned arrows. No mention had been made of the Panama Indians, but they were still there, primitive and savage. This was 1888, and even the Apaches were knuckling under—Geronimo was in exile in the Everglades—but the Panama Indians didn't keep up with the changing times. They were rumored to be headhunters, but that may have just been a nasty rumor.

"The direction the expedition will take is southwest." The colonel dipped the pen in the inkwell and drew a line on the map. It smeared because the nib was bent, but he kept his temper. "That's the railway. The company claims land on both sides of the line. It's heavily guarded, so the expedition will stay away from it."

Gatling was getting impatient with the colonel's palaver. "The expedition will be leaving from the Brooklyn Navy Yard?"

The colonel nodded. "The steam sloop *Jackson* will be leaving in the morning. You are to report by ten o'clock this evening. You have to be on board when your weapons are delivered. That will be sometime during the night. The opposition's spies have reported every damn thing about the ship, but they don't know about your weapons. They will be taken aboard by my guards. We don't want anything to happen to them before sailing.''

"They'd try to damage a Navy ship? They'd go that far?''

"Certainly they would. A small boat comes alongside, loaded with dynamite, in the dark. Navy torpedo boats are guarding the docks, but who knows? One well-placed charge could send the *Jackson* to the bottom, and there goes the expedition. It could be weeks, months, before they got it going again. If ever. The investors could get cold feet, as so often happens. Questions?''

"One big question, Colonel. If I'm to be the big gun, my big guns have to be available. Crated weapons won't be much good if there's a surprise attack. So they'll have to be out in the open and ready to fire. Speaking of weapons, what will I be testing this trip? I'll be taking weapons I know I can depend on, but what else?''

The colonel had been glum-faced; now he brightened up. He liked to talk about weapons; so did Gatling. Weapons were the only thing they had in common.

"Well, I can't tell you how enthusiastic I am about Maximite,'' the colonel said. "That's the new explosive I mentioned earlier. Fifty percent more powerful than dynamite. Lovely stuff. Think of how surprised Frobisher and Urbino's boys will be when you set off a few charges. But only if you have to, naturally.''

"Naturally,'' Gatling said, knowing goddamned well he'd have to use everything he had. And even at that, there was no guarantee that every member of the expedition, including himself, wouldn't die and rot in Darien.

"All you have to keep in mind is how powerful it is. Other than that, it's just like dynamite. Reduce the charge or the sky will rain bits of Gatling.'' The colonel looked at his watch. "You've got loads of time. Let's go and look at the other goodies.''

On the way to the solid-steel door that led to the three-story arsenal, the colonel said, "I'm afraid we can't demonstrate the mortar or the Maximite. Don't want to blow the house down, do we?''

Many of the colonel's questions didn't require answers. The

colonel unlocked the door, which opened without a sound, and there was the pungent smell of gun oil that Gatling liked so much.

The colonel liked it too. *"Eau de Maxim et Compagnie,"* he said.

"Bet your ass," Gatling said, going in first. "A mortar, you say?"

"Certainly not like the great monsters they used at the Siege of Vicksburg. You'll see. A new wrinkle on a weapon they've been using since the invention of gunpowder. Light. Light. Light. That's the ticket. Short, light, compact. Steel, not iron, no fuse to be lit. The mortar shell is activated when the shell slides down the tube and hits the striker. Do you follow me?"

"Sure. Has a shell ever exploded before it was fired from the tube?"

"Not very often. That was in the experimental stage. In answer to your next question, yes, the crewmen were killed."

"It takes two men to operate this drainpipe?"

"Not at all. One man can do it quite easily. Come on, man, I'll show you."

They got to where the mortar was. "As you can see, it's nothing more than a tube and a plate and a front support that can be adjusted, depending on what range you want. The base of the shell strikes the striker—sort of a firing pin—and the shell is fired. Over there is a box of Maximite."

The lid of the box had been pried open. Gatling took the pencil-thin stick the colonel handed to him.

"Used like dynamite," the colonel said.

"Sort of light for throwing," Gatling said.

"It wasn't designed for throwing."

"I might want to throw it."

"Then tie a rock to it. You'll find it quite useful, I'm sure. But this is what I wanted you to see."

The colonel pointed a bulky-looking rifle that lay on a box. "The Mondragon automatic rifle," he said. "Far from perfect, but I believe it to be the infantry weapon of the future. Not exactly a machine gun, though it's fully automatic. A slower rate of fire, for one thing. The slightly reduced rate of fire prevents it from overheating. It fires automatically as long as the trigger is depressed.''

"Looks like a vicious little bastard," Gatling said.

The colonel picked up the Mondragon automatic rifle. "It's a bit heavier than most military rifles," he said. "And it's innards are more complicated, naturally, but you'll like it when you get used to it.''

"Maybe I will.'' Gatling took the weapon and hefted it. Good enough balance for so long a gun. The colonel handed him the spring-fed magazine and he clicked it into the rifle.

"Try it," the colonel said. "On the man-sized target.''

A sheet of pine in the rough shape of a man stood against the back wall of the firing range. Gatling aimed and pulled the activating bolt. A stream of bullets jetted from the weapon. He fired off half the magazine before he released the trigger. He fired again until the magazine was empty. The thick wooden target was riddled with holes: belly, chest, and head.

"What's Maxim doing with a Mexican rifle?" Gatling asked. "I thought it was a deep dark secret.''

"Then you know about Colonel Mondragon and his rifle?''

"There's been talk in the business. Word always gets out. How did you get hold of it?''

"It fell off the back of a wagon," the colonel said. "Never mind how I got it. I got two. One is on its way to England. I'm sure Mr. Maxim will make his own improvements. Call it stealing if you like. To me, all's fair in love and weapons. It's odd for a Mexican to invent such a promising weapon. I thought they all sat around drinking tequila and strumming their guitars. When they aren't slaughtering one another, that is.''

"Some Mexicans can even read and write," Gatling said. Sometimes the colonel's disdain for brown-skinned people got to be a pain in the ass. At 60, he wasn't likely to change. The trick was to take him in small doses.

"Indeed they can," the colonel said heartily. "President Diaz is doing wonders for his country. It takes an iron hand, I always say, to rule such people. This democracy rot may be all right for the white races. However—"

"Better get going," Gatling said. "Wouldn't want to miss the boat."

Chapter
TWO

Gatling paid off the cab driver at the entrance to the Brooklyn Navy Yard. It was nine o'clock, and dark, and drizzling rain. Few lights showed on Pier 10, where he was going, but over at the next pier the biggest battleship he had ever seen was tied up and men were working on it under floodlights. Welding torches sizzled, throwing off sparks, and a traveling crane was lowering a gun turret into position. The workmen looked like black ants against the vast expanse of the great white ship.

Two Marines with Springfield carbines barred his way and told him to state his business. No, they didn't want to see the letter from Colonel Pritchett to Mr. Wheeler. The lieutenant would attend to that, and after a slight delay, the lieutenant came and read the letter. Then he looked at Gatling and asked him to remove his hat so he could take a better look.

"This way, Mr. Gatling," the lieutenant said, not knowing who Gatling was or how important he might be. He was young and might have succeeded in looking tough if he hadn't been so eager. A good word from an important man could lead to promotion. You never knew, and so you were polite and respectful until you knew a stranger was a somebody or a nobody.

Gatling didn't like him. He didn't like people who always had their eye on the main chance.

The dock was wet and greasy. Oil spills made colored patterns in the puddles. "My name is Tabor," the lieutenant said. "I'm told you'll be going with us."

"What else have they told you?" Gatling asked.

The steam sloop *Jackson* was dead ahead. Gatling could tell from its design that it was far from new. Sure as hell it wasn't the terror of the seas, but it would get them to Panama.

"Nothing," the lieutenant said nervously. "They told me nothing." He tried a laugh on for size. "Junior officers aren't told much."

Gatling told him not to feel left out.

Two more Marine guards were at the bottom of the gangway. Tabor snapped at them because they hadn't issued a challenge. They went through the motions while Gatling waited in the rain, holding the leather case with the modified light Maxim machine gun in it.

"Present arms," Tabor ordered, and they did that too. Gatling winked at the guards as he followed the lieutenant up the gangway. He wondered if Tabor was one of the gold-mining Tabors of Colorado. Could be. These rich snot-noses were always looking for a little glory before they became fat-assed behind a mahogany desk.

The *Jackson* was old, but it had been fixed up. Tabor led the way to a kind of anteroom where a young male secretary, a tall, languid man with thinning blond hair, slouched behind a desk with important papers on it. The colonel hadn't mentioned a male secretary. Gatling wondered how this male secretary would stand up to poisoned arrows.

Tabor told the secretary who Gatling was. He told Gatling the secretary's name. "I'm afraid Mr. Wheeler may not be available at the moment," Irby, the secretary said. "I'll see."

Gatling had an answer for that, but he kept it to himself. Working with the colonel had taught him to be patient, sort of. It wasn't easy, but he had been in the white world for a lot of years. He had been raised by the Zuni Indians, in New Mexico, after his parents were killed and scalped by marauding Apaches. The Zunis never lied, not even when what they said cut you to the quick. He liked the Zunis better than male secretaries.

In a moment Irby was back. "Mr. Wheeler will see you," he said, as if the President himself, or even the Pope, had said okay.

"Not you, Mr. Tabor," he told the lieutenant.

Gatling went into what must have been the captain's cabin. Where was the captain bunking? Gatling thought. Murdock Wheeler sat behind an enormous desk piled high with maps and papers. He had a glass in his hand. He was big and fair-haired and handsome. He had a red face, the kind of skin that doesn't brown. Some people might take the ruddy face as a sign of good health. Gatling knew it was booze.

"A pleasure to meet you, Mr. Gatling," Wheeler said, coming forward with his hand out. "I'm sure Colonel Pritchett —fine old gentleman—has told you all about our little expedition."

The walls were paneled in rich wood; everything looked new. Gatling decided Wheeler must have plenty of pull with the Navy Secretary. "I see you're admiring my appointments," Wheeler said, following up with a braying laugh. "Truth is, I've been using it as an office. Have to put on a show for the investors. Personally I'd as soon sleep in a tent. Give me the rough life anytime."

"Sure," Gatling said. If Wheeler slept in a tent, it would be pretty fancy. In cold climates there would be a duckboard floor with a rug on it, a patent stove to keep him warm. Gatling hadn't seen his personal cook yet, and wondered if he had a waxed mustache and a tall white hat. Just the same, Wheeler had done things. He wasn't about to downgrade the man because he was a hog for comfort.

Gatling took the colonel's letter from his pocket. Wheeler waved it aside. "No need for that, Mr. Gatling. Colonel Pritchett has told me all about you. You come highly recommended. Of course, while you're a member of my expedition, you'll take orders from me."

"Sounds reasonable. Do I get paid?"

Wheeler brayed another laugh. Gatling wondered if he'd been

raised around jackasses. But given his background—the best of everything, it was said—that wasn't too likely.

"No, you won't get paid. Colonel Pritchett is paying you, isn't he? But if everything works out, there could be a nice bonus that has nothing to do with the Maxim Company."

"I won't say no to that," Gatling said. "Mr. Wheeler, do you know what you're up against here?"

Wheeler got a bit redder in the face. "What the hell do you mean by that? Of course I know what I'm up against. The things I've done, the places I've been, and you ask me a question like that."

"Just a question, Mr. Wheeler."

"That's all right. I'm just a bit edgy, which isn't like me, Gatling." Gatling thought: If he calls me Gatling, I'll call him Wheeler. Wheeler wasn't just edgy, he was hung over.

"A lot depends on this expedition," Wheeler said. "And there are serious problems, I admit. Usually I have the complete support of some government or some group of financiers. All the money I want, all the men I need. This is all right"—his wave took in the paneled walls, the rich carpet—"but it could have been better. It took some arm-twisting to get this ship from the Navy. Twenty Marines, for Christ's sake! I can't see why our government doesn't just *seize* Panama and have done with it. Oh, well, mustn't complain."

It seemed to Gatling that Wheeler was complaining about everything. Was this showman-engineer making his complaints heard so he wouldn't look bad if he failed?

Gatling wanted to get down to brass tacks. "About the guns?"

"Yes, we'll be needing the guns," Wheeler said absently, as if he didn't want to talk about it. "In Cuba, General Pedro Weyler sent five hundred Spanish troops to protect my railroad from the *insurectos*. So safe I might have been building it across New Jersey. That's the kind of thing I like to see."

You won't see it in Panama, Gatling thought. Down there, a third of your Marines—a third was the accepted death rate—will die of disease or come down with a permanent case of the shits. A fighting man wasn't at his best when his guts were twisting with the pain of dysentery.

Wheeler got up and took a bottle of brandy from a liquor cabinet concealed behind dummy books. Behind a complete set of dummy Dickens he had at least a case of brandy, and he had an ice bucket and a soda siphon. He fizzed a little soda into his drink and sat down behind his desk. After he downed half the drink he placed his hands on the desk.

"Can you do it, Gatling?" he asked. "Can you get us through? Tell me what you think. I've been in the wildest places on earth, but I'm not a soldier, I'm an engineer, and a damned good one, as I'm sure you'll agree."

The big bastard wants me to hold his hand, Gatling thought. How old was he? The newspapers gave his age as 40. Maybe he was a few years older. Showmen of any kind liked to lop a few years off their age. Wheeler reminded Gatling of another showman he had known, a famous war correspondent who wrote up whatever war it happened to be from the safety of a whore's bed or the back room of a bar. In the past, kings and presidents had made life easy for Wheeler, but now he didn't have General Weyler's 500 soldiers—he had 20 Marines.

It would have been funny if it hadn't been so . . . what? What the hell, it *was* funny, but Gatling didn't crack a smile. He said, "My automatic weapons do the work of many men. That's what they're designed for. If nothing happens between here and the Maxim warehouse, we'll have enough heavy iron to stop an army."

Gatling pointed to the gun case. "There's a modified light Maxim machine gun in there. The gun and five belts of three hundred rounds. I've used it in . . . I won't say where . . . but there's no better man-stopper around. Want to see it?"

Wheeler sank the rest of his brandy and soda. "No, it wouldn't mean anything to me. Take it up with Mackenzie."

"Who's Mackenzie?"

"First lieutenant Everett Mackenzie. He's in charge of the military side."

"He won't be in charge of me," Gatling said. "And he won't be in charge of my weapons. I doubt if he knows a machine gun from a peashooter.''

Wheeler's face couldn't get any redder than it was. But he was angry. The drunk's quick switch from affable to nasty. He seemed to think it was time to put Gatling in his place. It had been tried by others, and Gatling's reaction was always the same. He walked out no matter what the cost.

''Mr. Mackenzie is an experienced officer,'' Wheeler said, rattling the ice in his empty glass. The glass was very large. Gatling was reminded of the old joke: Drunk: ''My limit is three drinks a day.'' Temperance Preacher: ''Yes. But you drink them out of a bucket.''

''He's fought Indians in the West,'' Wheeler said.

''So have I,'' Gatling said. ''The more you know about Indians, the less you know about Indians. Mister Mackenzie doesn't know Panama Indians. Nobody does. Beside the point. I'll do my best for you, but it has to be the way I see it.''

''Indeed?'' The friend of kings and presidents didn't like to be talked to that way. ''The hell you say.''

''Goodbye, Wheeler,'' Gatling said, picking up the case of Maxim. ''It's not too late to telephone Colonel Pritchett. He'll find a replacement by morning.''

Now both men were standing. ''I can have you detained,'' Wheeler said. ''I have the Department of the Navy behind me.''

''You have twenty Marines behind you,'' Gatling said. It was time to call this loudmouth's bluff. Panama wasn't the place to do it. ''You'll have blood on the carpet if you try to detain me.''

Wheeler sat down. Gatling figured he would. Wheeler said, ''Sit down, Gatling. Forget about Mackenzie. You'll meet him in due course. Now if you're half as good as you talk, we'll just waltz across Panama.''

''A slow waltz,'' Gatling said.

''I'd like you to get acquainted with the other members of the expedition. But first I'll have another quick one. Might as well. It's been a long day and there won't be much time for drinking where we're going.''

Gatling just grunted. He figured there would be a lot of drinking where they were going. Drunks drank. He wondered if Wheeler had a personal bartender as well as a personal cook.

Irby was still at his desk when they went out. Wheeler called him Irb, and Irb called Wheeler Dock. Very cozy and democratic, Gatling thought. Just as long as neither of them called him Gat. There was something odd about Irby, but he couldn't figure it out. Not all male secretaries were queers, though many were, but they were beginning to be replaced by women, and a good thing too.

"Hold the fort, Irb," Wheeler said.

Lieutenant Tabor was waiting in the passageway and he said, "I thought you might need me, Mr. Wheeler."

"That's very thoughtful of you, Mr. Tabor," Wheeler said. "Where would you like to start, Mr. Gatling?"

Gatling said with the Marines.

"Certainly, Mr. Gatling. But first don't you want to have your . . . er . . . luggage put in your cabin? It's right next door to a very pretty lady, even if she is a newspaper reporter."

Lieutenant Tabor laughed dutifully.

Gatling said, "I'll take care of my luggage." He wasn't about to let anyone lay hands on the gun case. "I'm told you have two reporters on board."

"Mr. Olds of the *New York Times,* is the other," Wheeler said. "Although I'd hardly describe him as a reporter. Fine man, fine reputation. Perhaps you recall his dispatches from the Franco-Prussian War?"

"What about Miss Morrison?' What wars has she been in?"

"Well, the right of women to vote has been one of them. But I know you'll find her most interesting. Miss Morrison works for Mr. Pulitzer's *New York World.* She's quite lovely, like her newspaper. Has a most pleasing aspect."

Wheeler raised his voice. "Can you hear me, Miss Morrison?" Then he whispered to Gatling, "Miss Morrison is always listening at keyholes."

"I heard that too, Mr. Wheeler." Miss Morrison came out of the shadows. "What's this pleasing-aspect sauerkraut? You make me sound like an ad for a cemetery lot. This must be Gatling the Great. Want a clove, Gatling?"

"No, thanks," Gatling answered. "I haven't been drinking."

"His jokes are better than your jokes," she said to Wheeler.
"Put 'er there," she said to Gatling, holding out her hand.
"Morrison—Sarah—is the name. A graduate of Hell's Kitchen
and proud of it. Forty-ninth and Ninth is where I come from.
Ever been over that way?"

Gatling liked her sassiness. "Sure. Got sandbagged there one
dark night."

"Probably by my father, Mike the Pike," Sarah Morrison
said. "Mike's up the river right now."

Wheeler brayed his loud laugh. "Miss Morrison's father is
State Senator Michael T. Morrison, and he's up the river in
Albany, leading the forces of progress and prosperity. Miss
Morrison is a graduate of Wheaton College, in Massachusetts."

"More's the shame," the lady reporter said, giving Gatling
a long look. "Gatling, my boy, has anybody ever told you you
look like Honest Abe?"

Coming from her, Gatling didn't mind the city talk. City
people talked like that to fill up the pauses. Not talking made
them uncomfortable. Nervous even.

Wheeler's last drink was drying in him. Suddenly he was
irritable, as drunks often were when the liquor wasn't flowing
fast enough. "Gatling wants to see the Marines," he said. "You
want to see some Marines, Miss Morrison? Or would you prefer
sailors?"

"I think you've seen more sailors than I have, Mr. Wheeler,"
she answered.

Something nasty was going on here, Gatling thought.

Wheeler looked ready to hit her. "What gives you the right
to talk to me like that?"

"Fifty thousand rights, Mr. Wheeler. Or reasons. You talk
your way and I'll talk mine. Any objections?"

Wheeler sucked in the wet sooty night air of Brooklyn coming
from the docks and put a lid on his temper. Gatling figured the
fifty thousand reasons meant fifty thousand dollars.

"Let's all of us be friends," Wheeler said.

Nice folks, Gatling thought.

He didn't get a good look at Sarah Morrison until they were

in the Marines' quarters. On deck, in the drizzle and dark, she was just a shape. Here under the lights she was something to see. She had better lines than the *Jackson*. Gatling thought of her as looking like one of the new, low-slung torpedo boats the Navy brass were bragging about. Sleek and sassy, plenty of power, loaded with steam, all push and go.

Gatling knew there wasn't a Marine there that didn't want to give her a good hosing. She looked like she needed a good hosing. He knew *he'd* like to give her a good hosing. Her hair was corn yellow, but she had clear green eyes. Emerald eyes. Slightly taller than the average woman, just right for a man who stood over six feet. She had high cheekbones, a pointed chin, sharp white teeth that gave her a catlike appearance. That's what she was, Gatling decided, a spoiled cat, and with all of the cat's cunning and self-centered nature.

Gatling got to meet First Lieutenant Mackenzie, two sergeants named O'Hara and Dobbs, and two corporals, McCain and Ehrlich. The privates had names like Finnegan or Kramer. Most were Irish or German, with a few Yankees or Southerners sprinkled among them. Not all were young.

Mackenzie wasn't young. He was long-faced and sandy-haired, and looked more like a lay preacher than a soldier. Gatling figured he had held high brevet rank in the Civil War, had been reduced to first lieutenant—and there he'd stuck. He didn't have much to say. He was silent rather than sullen. Gatling didn't ask him about fighting Indians. Marines didn't fight Indians. That was just something Wheeler had dreamed up. You never knew what drunks were going to say.

It was obvious that Wheeler was popular with the enlisted men. He had a different face for everybody, Gatling thought. The men whistled and cheered when Wheeler suggested to Mackenzie that they be given a tot of rum before they turned in for the night. Mackenzie acknowledged the suggestion with a nod, but didn't say yes or no. It didn't look as if he meant to break the rules, not even for a glad-hander like Wheeler.

The men were dressed in rough clothes. A lot of them would have been laborers if they hadn't been in the Corps. No rifles

were in sight. But even in their hobnailed boots and canvas suits
and canvas hats they still looked like soldiers. So all the dumb
secrecy was a waste of time, Gatling decided. He hoped
Mackenzie would break down and give them the tot of rum.
Not long after tonight, a third of them would be dead.

It was getting late, and some of Wheeler's party had gone
to bed. They passed a cabin with a DO NOT DISTURB sign
on the door. That was Bateman Olds of the *Times,* Wheeler said.
They got to the officers' mess, and someone there was playing
a piano while others sang. Behind the bar were portraits of
Presidents Cleveland and Jackson. The sloop was named after
Andy. There were two bartenders, but some of the younger
engineers and surveyors were behind the bar, making fools of
themselves. No ship's officers were present.

Wheeler, with another drink in his hand, told Gatling he would
meet Captain Decatur later. The showman brayed. "Not that
Decatur, not Steve. The captain's not that old." Gatling was
more than tired of Wheeler. It was April but it was too hot in
the lounge: too much noise, booze stink, and cigar smoke.
Mackenzie, who was being badgered by Sarah Morrison, was
the only one there who smoked a pipe. And he was the only
one who wasn't drinking.

Gatling got a stein of cold beer and looked for a place to sit
down for a few minutes. A long, thin man who looked far from
well beckoned him over to his table. It took Gatling a moment
or two to recognize Timothy O'Sullivan, the most famous Civil
War photographer after Matthew B. Brady—and he was famous
only to those who were interested in war photography. Gatling
was.

"Wheeler didn't bother to introduce us," O'Sullivan said.
"So I'll do the honors."

Gatling said, "I know who you are. My name is Gatling."

"And I know you too," O'Sullivan said as they shook hands.
"Otherwise I wouldn't have invited you over. I'd been told
you were joining us, but I'd heard of you before then. Like me,
you're well known in your own way."

"Not too well known, I hope," Gatling said. He liked

O'Sullivan. He had a faint Irish accent, a sardonic smile, cold blue eyes that had seen much death. Gatling wondered what a man in obviously poor health was doing in an expedition to Panama, one of the unhealthiest places on earth. But that was his business.

"Well known in your own line of work," O'Sullivan said. "Must be interesting what you do. Maybe you'll tell me about it sometime."

"Probably not, Mr. O'Sullivan."

"Then we'll say no more about it. Call me Tim if you don't mind. Well, now, what do you think of our little expedition? I mean *Mister* Wheeler, in particular."

Gatling looked at Wheeler, who was getting drunker by the minute. Leaning on the piano with a glass in his hand, he was leading the other merrymakers in a song.

"I think he's a horse's ass," Gatling said. "But maybe he's all right when he's in the field."

O'Sullivan took a long drink from his beer mug. "Don't count on it. You want some advice? Get off this tub before she sails. Matter of fact, get off right this instant."

Gatling looked around the smoky officers' mess. "Why don't you get off? Anyway, what's so bad about it?"

O'Sullivan shrugged. "In answer to your first question. I won't get off because I need the money, and besides, I don't give a damn. As to the second, what's wrong with this ship— this expedition—is *Mister* Wheeler. I know all the marvelous things he's done in the past. But that was then. A man ought to know when his best days are behind him."

"Hard to do, Tim."

"Sure it is, but a man shouldn't risk other men's lives because of stupid pride. I get the feeling he's completely unreliable. A man shouldn't be in command if he isn't up to it. But I don't want to put a damper on this lovely party. But don't say I didn't warn you."

Gatling just nodded. He didn't know what to make of O'Sullivan, but he liked him, all right. He had the look of a man who wasn't long for this world, and maybe that was why he didn't give a damn.

"Want another beer?" Gatling asked him.

"Ah, no, I've had more than I should. Besides, here comes Miss Morrison of Mr. Pulitzer's *New York Pisspot,* so I think I'll be off to my bed."

O'Sullivan got up unsteadily and swept off his old slouch hat in exaggerated gallantry. "Ah, the lovely Miss Morrison," he said, giving her one of his sardonic smiles.

"Hello, Tim," she said, but didn't smile back. She didn't look after him as he lurched away from her.

"What's Tim been telling you?" she asked Gatling, sitting down as if she'd been invited. The smell of whiskey and cloves came from her.

Gatling wondered why she bothered to chew cloves. Nobody chewed cloves unless they'd been drinking, and it was a dead giveaway. He put her age at 25. It was a bit young for a woman to be hitting the bottle.

"We were talking about the weather," Gatling said.

"He wasn't talking about death and man's mortality? I'd be surprised if he wasn't. He's dying, you know."

"He didn't get around to that," Gatling said. "We didn't talk about that. Look. I don't know the man. I know his work, that's all. Why should he tell me anything?"

She reached over and drank what was left of Gatling's beer. He didn't mind that; he could always get another beer. Yet there was something about it that annoyed him. Women who were close to a man did that all the time: picked at his plate, took a puff at his cigar, sipped at his drink. But this one thought she could do anything. The daughter of the rich and crooked Tammany politician!

"If O'Sullivan's dying, then let him die," he said. "He did something nobody else ever did and I respect him for that. What he's doing here is his business."

She frowned. "What's biting you, handsome?"

"Not a thing," Gatling said, getting up to walk to the bar for another beer. He brought back the stein of beer and a brimming glass of brandy.

"You want a clove to go with it?" he asked.

"Not even water," she said, not mad yet but getting close to it. Then she unspooled a bit. "Would a roll in the hay relax you, Gatling?"

"In exchange for what?'

"Information."

"Not tonight. I have a splitting headache," Gatling told her.

"Would a Seidlitz Powder help you?" she said, and they both laughed. "Looka here, Gatling, what's going on? I get the feeling something's going to happen tonight. What is it? The captain gave orders nobody on or off the boat after ten. You got here before ten."

Gatling took a sip of beer, thinking sure as shooting he'd like to put the hose to this green-eyed female. She thought she was the cat's ass, and she was in a way, but he was thinking of the weapons he was expecting from the Maxim warehouse. The weapons came first, and so did the job, and there was no difference between them. You couldn't let succotash get in the way.

"Come on, Gatling," Sarah Morrison said. "What's going on?"

"Ask the captain."

"I did ask him and he said Navy regulations. That's bullshit."

The bon-voyage party was beginning to thin out. One of the engineers was puking behind the bar and a steward was waiting patiently with mop and pail. Wheeler waved to Gatling as Irby and Lieutenant Tabor helped him through the door.

"Why didn't you ask Wheeler?" Gatling said. "There he goes. I know you two must share a lot of secrets."

That got her mad. "You know that for sure, do you?"

"Knew it right off. You learn to spot things, you been around as long as I have."

"You're as big an idiot as Wheeler," she snapped. "No, you're not. You're just trying to feed me birdseed. I did ask Wheeler, but he just winked."

"Maybe he had something in his eye?"

That didn't even get a smile. "Gatling, talk on board is you're some big troubleshooter from out West. No hard feelings, but I never heard of you till late this afternoon. Too late to do any digging."

"Nothing to dig," Gatling said. He was getting tired of the conversation. "Miss Morrison, it may be your job to ask questions, but I don't have to answer them. One thing I know about reporters is this. They'll do anything to make themselves look important. Most of them. I'm not thinking of myself. The lives of a lot of people are at risk and I'm not going to make it worse for them by talking to reporters. Once we're at sea I'll tell you anything you want to know."

"How could I get a story off this ship? Tell me that, you sanctimonious bastard." She finished her drink and banged the empty glass on the table. One of the stewards was clearing bottles and glasses off the bar. He looked over and told her the bar was closed.

"Mind your own business," she snapped at the man, who just shrugged and went on with his work.

Gatling looked at her. She was angry and pretty and a little drunk. He wondered what was eating at her. Maybe she didn't know herself. He guessed she was one of these newfangled women who had left the nest but hadn't learned to fly yet. The hell with that. There were things to be seen to.

He left her sitting there.

Chapter
THREE

The two wagons from the warehouse arrived about an hour before dawn. There was fog on the oily water of the East River, and except for the horn-tooting of a steam tug it was quiet. On the far side of the river lights winked through the fog. The city and the harbor hadn't come to life yet.

Gatling was on deck when he heard the wagons coming in through the gate. The iron-hooped wagon wheels rattled over the cobblestones of the dock. Mackenzie had gone to the gate to wait for the wagons. Now he came back with them. There was no one on deck except Gatling and the watch.

Mullins, one of the colonel's best men, was driving the lead wagon, and Gatling went down the gangway to talk to him. The hides of the horses were wet from the fog, and so were the canvas tops of the wagons. Mackenzie stood by without saying anything.

"What took you so long?" Gatling said to Mullins.

There were crates and armed men in both wagons, and the man sitting beside Mullins carried a sawed-off shotgun under his slicker. Mullins climbed down so he could talk to Gatling without being heard by the others.

"The colonel got word we were going to be firebombed on the way here," Mullins said. "His inspector pal in the police.

Only, the inspector didn't know where. Not much you can do about firebombs coming down from a roof, so the colonel told me wait. Anyhow, the colonel says, we don't want to fight a war in the streets.''

"What happened?"

"Took the inspector half the night to find the bastards and scare them off. Guess the stuff is safe enough now.''

"You did good," Gatling said. "Everything's been checked out?''

Mullins nodded. "Helped the colonel do it myself. We went over it twice.''

They got the wagons unloaded.. Everything was put in the _____ ' Mackenzie locked it and gave Gatling the key. ____ ?idn't ask any questions.

"I'd like a guard posted," Gatling told him.

Mackenzie showed no surprise. "I'll see to it.''

Gatling went to his cabin. Time enough to check the weapons after the ship was under way; it would give him something to do. The fog was lifting, but the sky was still dark. Out on the dark river there was more activity than there had been, but no more was being done on the great white battleship.

He was unlocking the door when he felt a smudge of something on the door handle. He looked at his hand, and even in the dim light he saw a faint film of oil. He thought he heard a muffled sound, but couldn't be sure. The ship was beginning to wake up, and there were sounds all over the place. A bell clanged and drowned out all the other noises until it stopped.

He listened at the door, and there was nothing. A quick turn of the key and a hard shove slammed the door open, and it hit the man standing behind it in the face. He was bent slightly forward and the heavy oak broke his nose, but he didn't cry out and he didn't drop the knife he had brought up for a downward plunge. The knife flashed down, and would have buried itself in Gatling's chest if he hadn't jumped back and smashed the killer's wrist with the barrel of the .45. This time he yelped and the double-edged knife dropped, and he was scrambling for it when Gatling belted him in the back of the head and he fell on the upturning blade. He screamed and kicked and fouled his pants, and then he died with Gatling's boot pressed down hard on his back.

There was shouting and running feet on the companionway, and Mackenzie came through the door with a Colt .45 in hand. Gatling had pulled the knife from the killer's chest and was looking at it. It was lodged so deeply, he'd had to pull hard to get it out. The knife was a stiletto, long-bladed, double-edged, and it came to a point. It was no good for anything but killing. A killer's knife. The little, dark-faced dead man on the floor looked like a killer. Gatling nodded toward the door and Mackenzie closed it.

"Somebody has it in for you," he said.

Gatling wiped off the blade on the little killer's coat. It was a good knife. He would keep it.

"Looks like it," he said. "But nothing personal. He was hired."

Mackenzie looked at the dead man. "Oh, sure," he said. "A paid assassin." Mackenzie's face was expressionless. "Must have snuck in after the wagons. I'll have a word with those guards."

Gatling didn't think he'd find anything of interest in the dead killer's pockets. All he found was two hundred dollars, twice the going rate for what they called The Big Job in the New York underworld. It looked like they wanted to make doubly sure that he never got to Panama. He was the weapons man and they wanted him dead.

Knuckles hit the door and a loud voice ordered, "Open up. Captain Farragut."

Gatling had talked to the captain earlier that morning. A short man with a barrel chest and a growling voice. With a scrubby beard and a pugnacious jaw, he looked a little like U.S. Grant, except he didn't walk around with a cigar stuck in his mouth. He turned in the doorway and told the men in the corridor to get the hell out of there.

"What the blazes! You kill this man?" he asked Gatling, who still had the stiletto in his hand.

"Tried to kill me, Captain," Gatling answered. "Fell on his own knife. This knife. No sneak thief, a hired killer. What we talked about this morning, the people who want to stop this expedition. What do you want to do? Send for the police? That will delay sailing."

Captain Farragut scratched his beard with one finger. "No," he decided. "No police. This is my ship and this happened on Navy property. You'll make a sworn statement and sign it and we'll put the body ashore. See that it's done, Mr. Mackenzie."

"Aye, aye, sir," Mackenzie said.

The captain left and Mackenzie said, "I'll get this place cleaned up for you. Good thing it's a wood floor 'stead of carpet. My Lord, what a stink in here. You'll probably have to appear at some sort of a hearing when we get back, that is . . ."

Mackenzie didn't complete the sentence. If they got back, Gatling thought.

Later, after he signed the statement and while his cabin was being scoured out, he stood on deck as the *Jackson* moved out into the harbor, heading for the Narrows and the open sea. It was good to get away from the smoke and stink of New York. No matter how many times he'd been there, he couldn't bring himself to like it.

What began as a foggy morning turned into a bright clear day with a stiff wind and a choppy sea. O'Sullivan, who had been making pictures since the sun came up, turned the work over to his assistant, a young fellow named Bigelow, and joined Gatling at the starboard rail. He looked even more haggard than he had the night before.

Off in the distance was the flat coast of New Jersey. "Only two thousand miles to go," O'Sullivan said. He had a long thin cigar in his mouth, another behind his ear.

"You want a match?" Gatling asked.

O'Sullivan shook his head. "Not supposed to smoke," he said. "I just chew on the damn things."

"Good for you, Tim."

"That's New Jersey over there," O'Sullivan said.

Gatling smiled at this peculiar Irishman. "All right, Tim. Let's not be telling me where New Jersey is. You want to know about the little bastard that tried to kill me. That's what happened. I might as well clue you in to the rest of it."

Keeping it short, Gatling told him about the bitter opposition to the proposed canal, the hiring of William Frobisher and his gunmen. "They're all vicious sons of bitches. Frobisher is worse than the others because he's smarter. Used to be a Regular Army officer. West Point. He knows what he's doing and that makes him dangerous. That's what's known. What we don't know is how many men he has and how soon he'll hit us."

"Christ Almighty!" O'Sullivan said, and then he started to laugh.

Gatling stared at him. "What the hell's so funny?"

"Damned if I know." O'Sullivan rubbed his hands together like a man who'd just won a lottery. "Sure I do. My doctor tells me there's no way I'll see my next birthday, which is six months away. No matter what I do, sez old Doc Altschuler, I'm maggot food unless I will my body to some medical college. Don't worry, Gatling, old man. Nothing contagious. A faulty pump is what I have. I've been trying to play it kind of safe— why rush into the hereafter?—but now I'm not so sure."

"About what, Tim?"

"Don't you see? Even if the old pump doesn't fail me, I'll probably get killed by one of these gunmen. Oh, I know about this El Tigre fella and his shit-shirt rebels, but I didn't figure on being killed by one of them. American gunmen are better shots. Don't say I'm not patriotic. Give me a light, for Christ's sake."

Gatling put a match to O'Sullivan's half-chewed cigar, and he sucked in smoke.

Gatling said, "Listen to me, you Irish idiot. You don't have to be shot, snake-bit, or die of the shits in Panama. A good chance you will, a good chance I will. Even so, it doesn't have to happen. Ten to one, it won't happen."

"You're on. What're you willing to bet? My money is on this Frobisher. But you know, maybe I shouldn't be making such a joke out of it."

"Maybe you shouldn't."

"Ah, don't go Presbyterian on me. A bit sour like me you may be, only there's no need to pull a long face. I'm thinking of the people aboard the ship who don't know what they face."

Gatling saw that Sarah Morrison was back on deck and not looking much better than when the *Jackson* sailed. She hadn't been completely sober then, and now she appeared to be seasick. But she'd get over it; only a few unlucky souls stayed seasick all the time.

Gatling said to O'Sullivan, "They all knew Panama was going to be no church supper, but Wheeler was warned about Frobisher. The man I work for told me that, and I believe him."

O'Sullivan was enjoying his cigar, puffing on it as if he expected someone to take it away at any moment. "I don't doubt he was warned," he said. "But if it happened after a certain time of day it would've been water off a duck's back. Fearless as a lion is our *Mister* Wheeler after he's been into the cider barrel. Could be this is his last go-round."

Sarah Morrison was giving them the evil eye from far down the rail. Gatling knew why she was burned at him. So maybe it was just him she was mad at, and not O'Sullivan. Still and all—and he didn't know a thing about it—he got the feeling that Sarah Morrison and O'Sullivan were more than casual acquaintances.

"What do you mean his last go-round?" Gatling asked. "I'd say there's nothing wrong with his pump."

"That's what I like about you," O'Sullivan told Gatling. "You've got no sympathy for showboaters like me. Not that I'm a fraud, mind you, but I do *sort of* look forward to the deep six. But we were talking about our leader, *Mister* Wheeler. No, there's nothing wrong with his pump. I say this may be his last go-round because there's been talk—well founded, I believe—that his last job—that railroad in Cuba—had some peculiar twists to it."

Gatling saw that Sarah Morrison, seasick or not, was edging her way down the rail.

"Financial twists," O'Sullivan added, starting on his second cigar. "Huge payments made to some Spanish general with a German-sounding name."

"Weyler," Gatling said. "General Pedro Weyler."

O'Sullivan frowned. "Then you heard about it too. Never mind. Half of this money paid to Weyler was returned to Wheeler. So the rumor mills have it. And there were other big-money finaglings. Of course, this country runs on bribery and double-dealing. Every brick in Boss Tweed's splendid courthouse cost at least five hundred dollars. But it's a fine building when all's said and done. The same can't be said for *Mister* Wheeler's Cuban railroad. Shoddy construction, poor materials. In short, he's no longer trusted to do a good job."

"Then how did he get this job?" Gatling asked. "More bribery?"

"Looks like it," O'Sullivan said. "I know for a fact that he was turned down by most of the bigwigs. So this time out he's got a lot of smaller men behind him. Minor politicians, a tugboat company, some southern California land speculators . . ."

"What are you two conspiring about?" Sarah Morrison said, coming up close. Some of her yellow hair had come loose in the wind and she kept patting at it. She was trying for arrogance without much success. It was hard to be arrogant and seasick at the same time.

O'Sullivan was enjoying her discomfort. It showed in the way he smiled at her. "You look especially lovely this morning, my dear Sarah."

"Go shit in your hat," she told him without much energy. "Gatling can hold the hat."

"A ribald suggestion, to be sure." O'Sullivan was born in Ireland but raised in upstate New York, and didn't have much of an Irish accent left, but he liked to trowel on the blarney when he was feeling malicious. "We weren't conspiring about a blessed thing. We were, in fact, talking about the first Battle of Bull Run, where Gatling here served as the youngest drummer boy in the Confederate Army. Isn't that right, me boy?"

"It was the second battle," Gatling said.

Sarah Morrison turned as if to walk away from them. "No,

I'll leave,'' O'Sullivan said quickly. "I wouldn't want the investors to think I waste my days gabbing.''

Sarah Morrison gripped the rail and stared at the sea. The coast of New Jersey had disappeared. Now there was nothing but sea and sun and salt spray carried back by the wind. Gulls were following the ship.

"The first day is the worst,'' Gatling said.

"Yes,'' she said. "I'll be all right tomorrow.''

It was chilly in spite of a bright sun in a clear sky. Below decks the engines vibrated as the small ship ran south. On the forward deck O'Sullivan and his assistant were taking a group photograph of the expedition's engineers. Some of them looked as if they would rather be in their bunks. That's where Wheeler was, Gatling figured, in his bunk.

"My father is one of the investors,'' Sarah Morrison said. "That's what Tim meant by that remark. That's the only reason I'm here. I wouldn't have my job with the *World* if Mike the Pike wasn't my father. Mike has plenty of political clout these days. He started out by clouting people with his fists.''

An impudent sea gull had perched on the rail, and its cruel beak reminded Gatling of Colonel Pritchett's nose. And the bird had the same merciless eyes.

"That's politics for you,'' Gatling said.

"I'd like to convince people that I'm not just a rich politician's daughter,'' Sarah Morrison went on. "Something worthwhile . . .''

Only you don't know what it is, Gatling thought. Her manner was subdued—suddenly it was—and he decided he liked her better the other way. Anyway, he'd always liked bitches a lot more than mealy-mouthed women. She might be trying to play on his sympathy. If so, she was scraping the wrong fiddle. He'd known women who had suffered years of misery without complaint. Once, out West, he'd met a young, once-pretty woman who worked a farm 18-hours a day while her husband, a legless veteran of the Civil War, sat on the porch and drank moon.

"You'll think of something,'' Gatling said.

She took her anger out on the sea gull. "Go away, you filthy scavenger!" she screamed at the bird. The gull flew away without a sound, but some of the engineers looked up and waved. O'Sullivan who was just about to take their picture, stuck his head out from under the black sun-cover cloth and shook his fist.

"You're getting the engineers excited," Gatling said.

"I'd throw something at you if I had anything to throw," she said.

Gatling had an answer for that. Throw yourself. But he kept it to himself.

"Sometimes I think you're more interested in my body than my mind," she told him.

It was hard to surprise Gatling, but he didn't expect that. He had known this one less than twenty-four hours. He didn't know her at all. Yet he had to admit to himself that she spoke the truth: He was more interested in her body than her mind. Mind? How could you be interested in another person's mind?

"Well, there's no reason why I can't be interested in both," he said reasonably. That wasn't bad, he thought. If she talked like that, then so could he. He could do without her, but why not? One thing or another, it had been too long since he'd had a good bed-rassle, and if he didn't do the honors the lady scribbler might jump off the stern.

As if reading his mind she said, "Do you mean that, Gatling? Do you really mean it?"

"A stack of bibles. Like that."

"How can I be sure?"

"Ask anybody. I can give you references."

She was in and out of Gatling's cabin until they were off Cape Hatteras. There she said she was going to devote the rest of the voyage to bringing her journal up to date. Gatling was sorry to see her go, and at the same time he was glad. She was a handful to make a man sit up and ask for more, but she was a handful. Late at night, lying in his bunk, he could hear her rattling away at the new Eagle typewriter she had brought on board. It had a bell that rang at the end of every line, and then there would be the ratcheting noise of the carriage as she pushed it back and started on another line. Or when she was thinking or maybe taking a drink for inspiration, there would be no sounds at all. A lot of, if not all, the men on board were after her or were interested in her, which meant the same thing, and they came to her cabin door mostly at night when they were horny or lonely or drunk or half drunk. Now and then she went off with one or all of them, and in the morning she knocked on his door and asked for a drink, which he had because she had left some bottles of brandy there, and then not quite sober, she complained about the insincerity of men in general.

Only once was there trouble, and it happened late one night when some of the sports decided that Gatling needed a little shaking up. Gatling was no killjoy, but he wondered why Wheeler didn't do something to get his people ready for the ordeal ahead. Most of the engineers, surveyors, geologists, and mapmakers were young, and they wanted to whoop it up before they had to buckle down and go to work. And that was fine for the first few days out of New York. Even so, all-night boozing wasn't the best preparation for the stinking, disease-ridden jungles of Panama. But nobody ordered them to take it easy, and it wasn't the captain's job because they were civilians and not under his control. Anyway, the way they saw it, they were just having a good time.

Gatling was drinking beer and reading a book on small arms the night they came singing to his door. It was late, but he wasn't sleepy. On the *Jackson* there wasn't much to do except sleep. He hadn't expected the sports to bother him. They knew something of his reputation as a hard man, and they knew he had killed the knifer at the Brooklyn Yard, and for the most part they steered clear of him. But now they had been drinking, and it must have been somebody's notion that he wasn't as tough as he was cracked up to be. Not that Gatling himself had done any of the cracking up—that was their own idea. He turned the page and hoped the clowns would go away.

But they didn't. The goddamned college marching song left off and somebody pounded on his door. A loud, drawling voice called out, "Hey there, you old hermit, think you're too good to associate with the common folk? Listen here, bad man, are you as bad as they say you are—or is that what your publicity agent says? Come on out. Join the party. Set us straight, you old desperado. Is it true you live on horseshoe nails and sulfuric acid?"

Gatling knew the voice. It belonged to a young engineer named Shillitoe, a loudmouth, a bully, a college prizefighter who was always sounding off about something. Even at breakfast, when everyone was quiet, Shillitoe made himself obnoxious. He insulted the stewards, who had to take it. He'd given another engineer a bad beating in what was supposed to be a good-natured bout of fisticuffs on the forward deck. He was a son of a bitch.

Gatling didn't want trouble, but he knew it wouldn't go away. If he didn't stop it right off, it would get worse. He couldn't shoot the son of a bitch: It would not have been the sporting thing to do. Jesus Christ, he thought, all he wanted to do was drink a few bottles of beer and read his book.

More pounding on the door. Shillitoe shouted, "We'd like to see the color of your small clothes, bad man."

In some college towns it was considered great fun to strip a man of his pants and turn him loose for the police to charge him with public indecency.

Gatling swung his legs off the bunk and yanked the door open. He left the Colt .45 in its holster in its bag. If you didn't wear it, you couldn't use it. There was no call for that.

Shillitoe was startled by the way the door opened, but he didn't step back. As big as or even bigger than Gatling, he was well muscled and confident that he could handle any man on the ship. The five drunks with him were drunker than he was. To Gatling they were just a bunch of young idiots playing follow the leader, and some of them had the grace to look embarrassed when they saw Gatling's face.

"You got a burr up your ass?" Gatling said to Shillitoe.

"That's what's bothering you, sonny, go see one of the doctors. Now get the fuck away from here, you stupid, drunken clown, or I'll plug up your asshole and make you shit through your mouth."

That was gutter talk and Gatling was good at it when he had to be. An old-time gunfighter had once told Gatling, "If they come at you ugly, you come back twice as ugly. Be like a tiger with a toothache. Sometimes it works."

It didn't work with Shillitoe. "You call me sonny, I'll call you old man. Fair enough. What're you going to do about it? Shoot me dead? Stick me with your knife? Strike me dead with your grim-reaper eyes? The thing of it is, can you fight like a man?"

Gatling wanted to knee Shillitoe in the balls, belt him to the floor, and then kick him in the face. But he kept his temper. They needed all the engineers they had, and maybe Shillitoe wouldn't be a bad man in a real fight. It wasn't true that all bullies were cowards.

"Let's get to it," Gatling said, wanting to get it over. "Only, nobody mixes in when you start to lose. I wouldn't want to be fighting six *gentlemen* at the same time."

He knew they wouldn't gang up on him, but he wanted them to feel his contempt.

"What kind of men do you think we are?" one of them said. A bleary-eyed young engineer with an oversized gray college button-over sweater with a big M on the chest. Gatling sort of remembered that his name was Midlander or Milliner.

Shillitoe made a mock bow, and Gatling walked past him and up the companionway to the deck. It was a calm, clear night without much wind. Sarah Morrison and O'Sullivan appeared before the knot of men reached the forward deck. This was where Shillitoe liked to show off. A ring-sized section of the deck had been marked in white chalk. Some of it had been washed away by windblown spray, but it was clear enough.

Shillitoe was pulling off his sweater and shirt. His broad chest was hairless but banded with muscle. He gave Gatling what was intended to be a pitying smile.

"What rules?" he said to Gatling. One of his friends was standing by with boxing gloves. "American rules? British?"

Gatling said, "No rules, no gloves, no time, no rounds. We fight till one of us goes down. That'll be you, pie-face."

O'Sullivan laughed as he stepped forward to take Gatling's shirt. But he didn't say anything.

Shillitoe was startled. "No gentleman fights like that." Some of the engineers laughed and Shillitoe's face grew dark with anger. Few of them liked him and he knew it. "No gentleman—"

"We'll fight my way or not at all," Gatling said. "You challenged me, remember? You forced it. You want to back off, it's all right with me. Make up your little bird brain. Or are you hoping the captain will stop it?"

"Why you . . ." Shillitoe's head snapped back as Gatling hit him in the mouth with a straight left. It was a sneak punch and Gatling put all his weight behind it. It shook Shillitoe to his shoes but didn't knock him down. Blood trickled from his mouth and his eyes narrowed in a dangerous rage, and he came at Gatling like a professional prizefighter. His left shot out and Gatling blocked it but took a hard right to the body. It was like being hit with a sockful of rocks. Shillitoe followed up with a flurry of blows that drove Gatling back until he was close to the white line. Shillitoe had the weight and he was twelve years younger. He moved in fast, and Gatling punched him in the belly, and Shillitoe yelled, "Foul," and while he was still yelling Gatling punched him again in the same place. His thick body began to jackknife, but he straightened up with an effort. He relied a lot on his left. It shot out again and hit Gatling's cheekbone. Shillitoe bored in with rights and lefts, trying to get set for the uppercut that would finish the fight. Gatling had seen him use it on the man he'd beaten so savagely. Shillitoe's opponent hadn't been a bad boxer, but he was good-natured and didn't have Shillitoe's meanness. Shillitoe had battered him until he was reeling, then dropped him with a ferocious uppercut.

Gatling watched Shillitoe's right. His left did most of the

work. He kept his right in reserve. Once, in the mess hall, Gatling had seen him hold up his right hand, had heard him call it "my mighty hammer."

Now he was edging in to use it. Gatling knew he couldn't stand up to a full-force uppercut. Few men could, not even professional prizefighters. Shillitoe probably pickled his hands in brine, punched sandbags to make them even tougher.

They circled. Shillitoe grinned, and Gatling knew he was getting set to make his big move. His left jabbed at Gatling's face, driving him back. The left kept coming at his face. He blocked and tried to counterpunch, but Shillitoe kept on driving him back. It would be over in a minute if he didn't do something. The left hit him again and the right came up with incredible speed, so fast he could barely see it. He jerked his head back and it missed. Shillitoe cursed and tried to recover his balance. The force of the blow had thrown him off-center. They clinched for an instant and when they broke Gatling hooked his foot behind Shillitoe's ankle and brought him down hard. Gatling kicked him in the stomach when he tried to get up. He yelled, "Foul!" and lurched to his feet. Gatling beat him back to his knees, then sent him crashing to the floor with a savage blow to the side of the head. Shillitoe was conscious, but he couldn't get up. Two men lifted him and stood him on his feet. He stood there swaying on wobbly legs, and he would have fallen if the two men hadn't caught him in time. His mouth twisted, but no sound came out.

Finally he mumbled, "You're no gentleman, you son of a bitch!"

The two men pulled him away, thinking maybe Gatling would hit him again. No call for that, Gatling decided. The fight was over.

O'Sullivan handed him his shirt. "The young gentleman thinks you're no gentleman," the Irishman said.

"I hope not," Gatling said.

Chapter
FOUR

They reached the mouth of the Mono River at the hottest part of the day. Mono meant monkey in Spanish. On both sides of the river, the country was flat and the jungle grew right down to the water's edge. Even here, at the wide estuary, the river was sluggish and it spread out to form tidal marshes before it flowed onto the sea. Crocodiles disturbed by the ship's engines slid down into the muddy brown water. A hot wind coming off the land brought with it the stink of rotting vegetation. The sun was a shimmering brass ball in the pitiless blue sky. Except for the crocodiles, there was no sign of life.

There were sandbars at the mouth of the river, and they had to go ashore in small boats. Gatling and the Marines went first to cover the others in case of attack. Captain Farragut scoffed at the idea of an attack, saying the *Jackson*'s guns would blow the bastards to hell and gone if they had the temerity to fire on a party of Americans disembarking from a ship of the United States Navy. Gatling was nowhere as sure as the captain. On shore there was enough cover to hide a small army. Frobisher, if he decided to do it, could hit hard and fast and vanish into the jungle before the *Jackson* could bring its guns into play.

Even here, with a strong land breeze, mosquitoes were biting by the time they splashed up onto the beach. The Marines had smeared their faces and necks with some kind of medicinal grease provided by the doctors. Gatling had passed on that because he knew it wouldn't do any good. Until they came up with something better, the only thing that offered any protection was mud.

Gatling carried the modified light Maxim machine gun and 600 rounds of .303 ammunition in two canvas belts. The Marines were armed with single-shot, breech-loading Springfield carbines. Good, dependable weapons, but far behind the times.

They moved up the beach to the edge of the jungle. Monkeys screeched at them from the trees. Gatling carried the light Maxim at his hip, the first belt pushed into place and ready to fire. The second ammunition belt was linked to the first, making it possible to fire 600 rounds without interruption. Unless the light gun jammed. But it had never jammed in all the places he had used it. Of all the weapons manufactured or distributed by the Maxim Company, this was the one he liked best.

Mackenzie sent two men ahead, and when they came back they said there was nothing but monkeys in there. Under the trees it was steaming hot and the mosquitoes were ferocious. "Fuckin' doctors don't know nothin'," one of the Marines complained, slapping at his neck.

It took nearly two hours to get the civilians and the equipment ashore. They sure as hell had a lot of equipment, Gatling thought, watching the small boats coming in through the surf. Boxes of spirit levels, gradiometers, surveyors' compasses and chains, aneroid barometers, mercurial barometers, telescopes. The supplies bulked just as large: thousands of pounds of canned goods, beans, coffee, bacon, butter, whiskey. And the doctors had their quinine, surgical instruments, splints, and bandages.

Sarah Morrison came ashore in stiff white cotton, laced boots, and sun helmet. She wore a .38 double-action Ivor Johnson revolver on a plain brown belt without bullet loops. Gatling wondered if she knew how to use it. She was taking along too much gear: two big leather bags, the Eagle typewriter in its huge wooden, leather-covered case. Two young engineers acted as porters, and maybe they thought that would get them something. Bateman Olds of the *Times,* a stooped, gloomy man with white hair, had just one bag, and he carried it himself.

The grease the doctors had smeared on Sarah Morrison's face was starting to drip from her chin. It stained her white coat and she looked mad. She was vain about her looks, Gatling knew, but this was the last place on earth for vanity. Here there was nothing but heat and stink and gibbering monkeys. They didn't call it the Mosquito Coast for nothing. Sarah Morrison had the thin, fair skin that mosquitoes like, and before the day was over she would be covered with lumps.

The *Jackson* sailed. Gatling knew there wasn't a person there that wasn't sorry to see it go. He was sorry himself. On board the sloop there had been a soft bed, cold beer, fair-to-middling coffee, and no mosquitoes. Like all men who had battered around, he didn't enjoy the rough life for its own sake. Only Eastern dudes with money went in for that sort of bull.

Bright green mountains rose up about ten miles back from the sea. Before they left the beach Wheeler called a conference of what he called his "senior men," which included Gatling, Mackenzie, and Tabor. Wheeler unrolled a map on a rubber groundsheet, and it did show what the map described as "hills," but anybody could see that the elevations were wrong. The hills were mountains. They were high mountains. Gatling wondered how old the map was. Old maps were notoriously inaccurate, especially those made in the early days of exploration. These maps were copied and recopied, and sometimes new features were added for good measure.

Like the Lost Dutchman Mine, Gatling thought.

Wheeler's map had a pass marked on it. It might be there or it might not. But Gatling didn't say that, and neither did anyone else. They would just have to wait and see. Sarah Morrison looked distressed at all this vagueness and indecision. Bateman Olds, the old newspaper warhorse, just made a sour face. Gatling guessed Olds was accustomed to vagueness and indecision.

"These ruins," Wheeler said, jabbing at the map with a

pencil. "These ancient Indian ruins is where we will make camp tonight."

Gatling looked at the map. So did everyone else. The ruins were marked as lying between where they were and the foot of the pass.

Mackenzie said what Gatling was thinking. "Mr. Wheeler, these ruins, we should get to them before it gets dark. If they . . . if anybody should be laying in wait for us . . . we don't want to engage them in the dark."

Wheeler said confidently, "A point well taken, Mr. Mackenzie, but I don't think there's going to be any trouble. In fact, I doubt if there will be any trouble from here to the Pacific. After all, we're Americans. The day is past . . . however, as I say, your point is well taken and we must push on."

They pushed on through the stink and the heat, with the mosquitoes swarming around their heads and the monkeys screeching at them from the trees. The Marines suffered most because they had to carry the equipment and the supplies. No matter where they served, Gatling thought, the enlisted men always got the shitty end of the stick. Before they left the ship the doctors, fortyish men named Hazen and LaPlante, had dosed everyone with quinine, which usually worked against malaria, but not always. Somehow Gatling had missed malaria. Once you got it you never got rid of it no matter how long you lived.

Now they were about four miles from the ruins. So said the map. The same map that said high mountains were hills. Beating down on the wild tangle of green over their heads, the sun turned the rain forest into a steambath. Sarah Morrison drooped as she walked. Her crisp white tropical suit was dirty and sweat-soaked, and there was a desperate look in her emerald eyes. Walking beside her, Bateman Olds just put one foot in front of the other, taking his time, sweating far less than the others.

No one knew where they were going. No one had been there before. O'Sullivan said to Gatling, "This godblasted place looks like the first day of Creation. But the Garden of Eden it's not. Dismal is the only word that describes it." Gatling told him to fall back and join the civilians. "You call me a civilian," he complained. "I've seen enough battlefields to qualify as a monument."

"Fall back," Gatling repeated.

They made fairly good time until they came to a long stretch of swampland that was too wide to be skirted and had to be crossed. Inflatable rubber boats were used to float the boxes of equipment through the swamp. Up to his middle in black, stinking water, Gatling stayed close to the boxes that carried his weapons and ammunition. In places, some of Mackenzie's men had to clear the way with machetes. There were snakes, but nobody was bitten. The sun was going down by the time they reassembled on dry land.

Everybody was wet and dirty and hot. They rested and drank tepid water from their canteens. There was plenty of bottled water, but after that gave out the water they drank would have to be boiled. Gatling figured Wheeler had more than water in his canteen, because he was as boisterous as he had been that first night in Brooklyn. The ruins were dead ahead—they could be seen with binoculars—and Wheeler took that as a good sign. Gatling glassed the ruins, and they looked as if they were grown over with a thousand years of jungle. He suggested to Wheeler that they make camp where they were and head for the ruins in the morning. Wheeler said no. They'd move on in a few minutes.

"At least let Mr. Mackenzie's scouts take a look," Gatling said.

Wheeler agreed to that. An hour later the scouts returned and said the ruins were deserted except for monkeys. Gatling and the Marines moved out ahead of the others. It was quiet except for the drone of the mosquitoes; the monkeys didn't make noise after dark. It wasn't quite dark, but it was close enough; the light was thick and it was hard to see. Moving through unknown, possibly hostile country after dark was a bad idea unless there was a compelling reason. Here there was none: Wheeler just wanted to prove who was in command of the expedition. Mackenzie didn't like it any more than Gatling did, but he had to follow Wheeler's orders.

The ruins were spread out over five acres of land, and all but the highest points were tangled in wild vegetation. At some time in the remote past a village or town might have existed on the edge of the great buildings and monuments. If so, it had crumbled away and been buried and forgotten. The moon came out, and they could see great, flat-nosed stone faces in the pale, yellow light.

Gatling heard some of the Marines whispering, and he knew how they felt: This place scared them and they weren't thinking of hired gunmen who might be waiting to kill them. Wheeler and the others were hanging back, and maybe Wheeler was losing some of his bravado. Gatling whispered to Mackenzie, "I'm going to circle around and come in from the other side."

"You want to take some men?"

Gatling didn't want to do that; they would make too much noise. "The light gun is all I need," he answered. "If there's nobody there I'll come out through the ruins. Tell your men not to shoot me. I'm not telling you your job, but—"

"That's all right," Mackenzie said. "We'll handle it the way you said. We'll attack if you bite off more than you can swallow."

"Make some noise but hold back. You could lose half your men if they're already in position. No blame to your scouts. Frobisher—whoever—could've pulled back when he heard them coming. Plenty of time to come back after they left."

Mackenzie nodded. "That would be the way to do it. How long do we wait?"

Gatling got the point. He could be knifed or overpowered out there in the dark. "Twenty minutes," he said. "If you don't hear something by then . . ."

They were about a quarter of a mile from the ruins, too far not to be seen or heard unless forward scouts had been posted. That's what Frobisher would do, though he probably would keep the night-crawlers closer to his position. Scouts could give away a position if they weren't used right. Gatling always worked with what was possible. Frobisher and his men might be nowhere close; it was also possible that they were right there in the ruins.

Moving quickly but carefully, Gatling went out wide until he was about two hundred yards south of the ruins. Then he stopped and listened. All he heard were nighttime jungle noises. No jungle was ever completely quiet; something was always moving, chittering, snuffling, crawling. He went on, avoiding boggy patches of ground. If the light gun got fouled by mud, he wouldn't be much use to Mackenzie or to himself. He hoped Mackenzie's men weren't being too obvious; any experienced night fighter would recognize too much noise as a diversion.

He carried the light gun by the forward handle and the pistol grip. A single shot activated the gun and it became fully automatic. He kept his trigger finger away from the trigger in case he stumbled. In his pocket he had five pencil-thin sticks of Maximite, a match case, a long cigar. He hoped he wouldn't have to use the Maximite. No good letting them know everything he had. But he'd bring the ruins down on top of them if they were too well dug in to be killed by the Maxim.

Now he was far back behind the ruins, and from there he could see the great bulk of the temples, or whatever they were, and he started to move in because there wasn't that much time left. He edged his way through stone blocks tangled in yellow-green vines that looked like twisting snakes in the moonlight.

He climbed higher. The displaced blocks of stone were like a staircase. If they were in there, they had nobody guarding their rear. That wasn't something an ex-officer like Frobisher would neglect to do. Gatling was beginning to think he was dead wrong when he heard a faint noise. It might have been a rifle barrel scraping on stone. It could have been a branch creaking in the wind. But it was something.

He climbed as high as he could get, and below him was a sort of square surrounded by ruined buildings on all sides. The building at the far end of it had collapsed to its foundations. It looked down at the jungle where Mackenzie and his men waited in the dark. Gatling stayed still, watching for movement. The far end of the square was in deep shadow and it took a while for his eyes to get used to it. Then he saw it, something moving in the shadows. Just a slight movement, and then it stopped. He waited, and then it moved again. Something else moved, and it was too big to be an animal. No sounds reached up to where he was.

He steadied the light gun and opened fire, the activating shot followed instantly by the rattle of bullets flashing from the muzzle as he moved the gun from right to left. Men screamed and yelled. Gatling had no clear targets: He was depending on sheer firepower. Firing in spaced bursts so as not to overheat the barrel, he swung the light gun back and forth. Men were dying down there; no way to tell how many he had killed. He kept on firing. The second linked belt moved smoothly into the feed. Some return fire came at him, but it was feeble and erratic. He heard somebody yelling, "Get out! Get out of here!"

They tried to break out into the square, but he drove them back with bullets. Two bursts left dead men sprawled in the moonlight. Blocked by the Maxim, they were blocked by Mackenzie and his men on the other side. Careful not to damage the light gun, Gatling jumped and crawled and slid down to the square. Then he ran across it and out through a gap in the wall to give Mackenzie support. Down the slope from the ruins the gunmen had taken cover and were trying to make a fight of it. Gatling could see where they were by their rifle flashes. He moved down the slope firing from the hip. The light gun had a kick, but he was strong enough to control it. The light gun rattled . . . stopped . . . rattled again. Below him the last of the gunmen turned to face the deadly gun. A few tried to run, and he cut them down. Only three were left. One lay wounded. The other two had their hands up. Gatling covered them while Mackenzie and his men closed in from two sides.

"Well, now," Mackenzie said calmly. "What have we here?" He told Gatling his only casualties were two men slightly wounded. Gatling nodded. Two men wounded wasn't so bad, though any wound in this pesthole of a country could be fatal. Still, they had doctors. He was glad he wouldn't have to beat the shit out of Wheeler. Mackenzie might have to observe the rules. He didn't.

Mackenzie sent men into the ruins; a few skulkers might still be in there. "See to the wounded if there are any," he ordered. "We don't want them to suffer."

The men understood what he meant; this wasn't the time or place to be taking prisoners. "What do you want to do with these fine fellows, Mr. Gatling?" he asked, meaning the two men who had surrendered.

Gatling looked at them. They were Americans, one short, one tall, both about thirty. The wounded man had died without a sound. One of the prisoners, the short one, was bald and he wore a beard to make up for it. For a killer, he wasn't a bad-looking fellow. The other prisoner, the tall one, was ugly as sin. A stringbean with a wall eye, jug ears, and a weak chin.

"I don't know what I want to do with them," Gatling told Mackenzie. "You know what I'd like to do."

"Ah, you can't do that, Mr. Gatling," Mackenzie protested. "You can't just kill them. They surrendered, they're our prisoners."

"Guess you're right." Gatling decided that Mackenzie was a pretty good actor.

Three shots rang out in the dark ruins. "They're better off out of their misery." Mackenzie's voice was as bland as a deacon's. "But these two men don't have a scratch on them. We'll hold them till we find some kind of law."

Far below, at the edge of the jungle, Wheeler was yelling, but he was too far away to be understood. Tabor was supposed to keep him there until Mackenzie told him otherwise. Gatling knew he had to hurry it up: He didn't want to kill the prisoners in front of Tabor or Wheeler or the others. Bateman Olds might write it up in the *New York Times*.

"What law?" Gatling said. "We're not going to find any law."

Mackenzie asked, "Then what do you propose to do? Turn them loose?"

"We can't kill them, and we can't drag them clear across Panama." Gatling pointed a finger at the short man. "Where's Frobisher? No bullshit now. You don't owe him a thing. Say where he is. That's your ticket out of here."

"Don't tell him," the other man cut in, ugly and defiant. "He'll kill us anyway."

Gatling slapped the ugly man across the mouth, and Mackenzie thumbed back the hammer of his Army .45.

"Mouth shut, hands behind the head," Mackenzie ordered.

"You won't kill me?" the short man said. "I got to believe you. Frobisher's on his way from Colon. That's what Cleary told us. Cleary came down here first. Get things organized. Recruit some of the boys in Colon."

Gatling knew that Colon, on the Caribbean side of the Isthmus, was a haven for wanted men. "Where's Cleary now?" The name didn't mean anything to Gatling.

"Dead," the short man said, looking at the light gun. "You killed him with that."

It was nearly time. "How did Cleary know where we were?" Gatling reckoned he would get no straight answer to that. But it was worth asking the question.

"I swear I don't know," the short man said desperately. "I'd tell you if I did. Look, mister, it was nothing personal, us being here. Not me anyhow. Was broke, needed the money. We . . . you won't go back on your word?"

Gatling shook his head. "Get going, you and this ape here. Come at us again and I'll cut your balls off. Move before I change my mind."

They were ten feet away, walking fast, when Gatling shouted, "Stop or I'll shoot!" They didn't have time to run or duck or beg. He shot them in the back and they dropped like stones.

Prodding the spent shells out of the cylinder of the Colt, he said to Mackenzie, "They tried to escape. Dumb thing to do."

"You had no other choice, Mr. Gatling," Mackenzie said. "I know you hated to do it. But you'll get over it in time. Now I think we should tell Mr. Wheeler it's safe to come up."

Mackenzie sent one of his men down to fetch Wheeler and the others.

"That's a dandy little gun you have," Mackenzie said. "We'd have been in a real fix if not for you and the gun. Lord! I never saw or heard anything like it."

"There isn't anything like it," Gatling said.

Wheeler and the rest of them staggered up the hill from the jungle. The sports looked dead serious; even Shillitoe was subdued, there in the presence of so many dead men. Wheeler had been nipping, and smelled like it. Sarah Morrison had no expression on her face. This was the real thing, not just some stunt for the *New York World,* a newspaper that pulled many stunts. Irby stood behind Wheeler as if to give him support.

"How many were there?" Bateman Olds asked. The *Times* correspondent might have been asking the time of day.

Wheeler interrupted before Mackenzie could answer. "Who were they? Will somebody please tell me who they were?"

Gatling said, "William Frobisher's men. We talked about it."

"Yes, I know. But I hardly thought—"

"You see them," Gatling said. "Some hard case called Cleary recruited them. Cleary's dead, but Frobisher's on his way from Colon with men from the States. They'll be better men than these. Cleary picked them up in the Colon *cantinas.*"

Wheeler didn't want to listen. "All right, you've told me. We'll have to be better prepared, that's all."

Gatling couldn't let that go. "Mr. Mackenzie and his men were well prepared."

Wheeler said, "All right, Gatling. All *right!*"

Gatling said, "The men that talked about Frobisher may have been lying. Frobisher could be anywhere. Up ahead waiting for us maybe."

Bateman Olds said, "He told you about Frobisher but he's dead now?"

"Tried to escape, Mr. Olds."

"That's right, Mr. Olds," Mackenzie said. "Mr. Gatling had to shoot him. He was quicker than I was."

"I see," Bateman Olds said.

Wheeler wanted to get at Gatling. "You should have kept him alive so we could question him further. Get more information out of him. I'm holding you responsible for that, Mr. Mackenzie."

"Certainly, Mr. Wheeler," Mackenzie said.

Wheeler looked uncertain, as if he realized that he was getting on the bad side of the two men he had to depend on most. Tabor was more desk officer than fighting man, good for social occasions, good at smoothing things out, but even Wheeler must have been aware that he wouldn't be much good in a real fight.

"We'll say no more about it," Wheeler said grudgingly. "You've had men wounded?" The big man was concerned about the welfare of the little fellows. Mackenzie told him the two men would be all right. Wheeler nodded sagely. "That's fine. Good men, the best. Are we to spend the night in the ruins? What about the—"

"My men are taking care of it," Mackenzie said, meaning his men were getting rid of the bodies. "It'll be quite all right, sir. It's a good position. We can hold it against anything."

It pleased Wheeler to hear that. "Right you are, Mr. Mackenzie. That was my idea in the first place."

"A very sound idea," Irby, the secretary, said. Lieutenant Tabor nodded his agreement. No one else said anything because it was plain to one and all that Wheeler had come close to getting them killed. If Cleary's gunmen had wiped out the Marines, the rest would be dead or dying by now. They could run, but the killers would find them.

Sergeant Dobbs reported that the ruins had been cleared. For once the engineers and surveyors had to carry their own equipment. Mackenzie's men were needed to secure the position. The two wounded Marines were able to walk. One had been hit in the arm and the bone was broken. Dr. LaPlante, one of the expedition's two doctors, said he would try to save the arm. He would know by morning. The other Marine had a bullet crease along the side of his head. He was very young and tried to pass it off as nothing. "I cut myself worse shaving," he told the doctor. The doctor told him not to be such a goddamned fool.

Wheeler couldn't get his tent up because the square inside the ruins was paved with stone. So the great engineer had to make himself comfortable any way he could. Irby fussed around him, laying out blankets and inflatable pillows. Wheeler's private cook began to prepare a meal on an alcohol stove. A morose Swiss who never said anything, he kept to himself. Wheeler and Irby called him Fritz.

The engineers and surveyors had their own cook; the Marines cooked for themselves. Mackenzie came back after checking the guards, who were placed high in the ruins. There would be two shifts of guards, and everybody but the wounded men had to turn out. Mackenzie was taking no chances on a night attack.

Gatling stood a four-hour watch, then slept beside the light gun. But he didn't have to use it.

Chapter
FIVE

In the morning, everyone got two grains of quinine and a tablespoon of whiskey, the standard dose for malaria. There was nothing the doctors could give them for the other diseases and fevers rampant in Panama. Gatling got his quinine from Dr. Hazen, but said he didn't want the whiskey. It was too hot for whiskey.

The doctor shrugged. A sour-faced man of 50 or so, he had the weary air of someone who knows he is fighting a hopeless battle. "You don't drink whiskey, others drink too much," he said.

The Marine with the shattered arm had been feverish during the night. The other doctor, LaPlante, told Mackenzie the arm would have to be amputated.

Mackenzie got his men to put up a lean-to in a corner of the square. "Doc doesn't think he's going to live," he told Gatling. "A damned shame if you ask me."

Gatling ate breakfast with Mackenzie and the Marines who weren't standing watch. Tabor ate with Wheeler and Irby. Two scouts sent out early came back by the time breakfast was over. They had gone all the way to the foot of the pass without encountering any hostile activity. Under the lean-to the doctors were sawing off the wounded man's arm. The rasp of the surgical saw seemed loud in the hot morning silence. Mackenzie told Gatling none of his men had ever seen action. "No wars these days," he said. The sound of the saw was faint, but it bothered them and they tried to cover it with loud talk, even nervous jokes.

Gatling was checking his weapons when the two doctors came out from under the lean-to, drying their hands with towels. The amputation was successful, but the Marine was suffering from shock, low blood pressure, and fever. No way to tell if he'd live or die. They would have to wait and see.

Wheeler put on a stern face when he heard the news. "The price of progress. We all serve in our own way, I suppose. Do what you can, gentlemen."

Done with this little charade, he said this was the day when they'd get down to work. Little work had been done between the sea and where they were now. The country was flat and featureless, nothing much to make note of. The surveyors had taken some measurements, the mapmakers rudimentary sketches, and that was all. But now the mountains and the pass lay ahead, and it was time to get busy.

"This will be our headquarters until tomorrow," Wheeler said. "Today we'll work up to the top of the pass. In the morning we'll move on." He turned to the doctors. "Gentlemen, can the patient be moved by tomorrow?"

Dr. LaPlante, who had performed the amputation, said he didn't know. "He's very weak. If he's to have any chance, I think it will take longer than that."

Wheeler stuck out his chin like a man of decision, one of those strong-willed men who give talks to business clubs. Gatling could see how he'd be pretty good at raising money. Businessmen who never did anything but sit behind a desk would be intimidated by his stories of raw adventure in savage places. And their wives would like him. They'd all like him fine as long as he stayed sober.

"We'll discuss it later," he told the doctors.

Wheeler said they'd start in 30 minutes, enough time for Gatling to finish oiling the Mondragon automatic rifle and put it away. In Panama, especially in this part, everything metal grew a green-yellow mold in a few days, if you didn't look after it. In fact, everything rotted whether you looked after it or not. Cloth, leather, rubber—everything rotted. Rot set in faster when it rained, and when it rained it went on for days, sometimes weeks. Things rotted, and so did people.

Mackenzie stayed behind. He hadn't slept all night. He had to sleep. Tabor and ten Marines were to provide protection for Wheeler and his subordinates. So was Gatling. O'Sullivan was coming along to take photographs. Sarah Morrison and Olds decided to remain in camp.

It hadn't rained yet, but it looked like rain. It wasn't the rainy season, but with mountains so close, it could rain at any time of year. Wheeler wore a bright blue shirt, rubber shoes with canvas tops, a straw sombrero with a floppy brim. Gatling thought he looked very picturesque, like an illustration in a magazine of travel and adventure. He wore a nickel-plated Colt .45 double-action and a cased machete with a fancy handle. Both were slung from a broad leather belt with silver stitching.

Here was a man's man, the weapons seemed to say. O'Sullivan posed him for several pictures, which pleased him no end. Gatling knew Wheeler didn't like O'Sullivan, but the Irishman's camera could add to his fame, so he was prepared to put up with a reasonable amount of sarcasm and disrespect.

It took hours for Wheeler and his men to work their way to the foot of the pass. The heat got worse as the day dragged on. Gatling, a sergeant named O'Hara, and three men went up to the top of the pass to see what was on the downslope. The pass was about 600 feet above sea level—so the engineers said—but all they saw were more mountains and more jungle, with the Mono River a dull silver straggle to the south. If Frobisher was out there, he wasn't showing himself. No sign of life. No movement of any kind.

Mountains rose up on both sides of the pass; it wasn't quite as hot as it was in the jungle. The Marines were glad to just watch and wait. Nobody had anything to say. Panama had a way of weighing down on people, Gatling thought. Maybe it was because *something* was always trying to kill you.

Wheeler and his men reached the top of the pass by late afternoon. Though there was no need of it, Tabor brought the men with Gatling to attention. The civilians were tired and glad to sit down for a while. They drank water and fanned themselves with their hats. Gatling saw that Shillitoe's swollen, battered face was getting back to its normal shape.

Wheeler wasn't tired. He'd been nipping, though he wasn't drunk. "At ease, men," he told the Marines.

The Marines didn't budge until Tabor told them to. Wheeler said to Gatling, "We've been working while you fellows were taking your ease up here."

"Sure," Gatling said. What could you say to a man like Wheeler? What the hell! He was being paid to protect the son of a bitch and he would do it. It was just a job. He wondered what the colonel would say if he returned to New York and reported that Wheeler had been carried off by a crocodile.

Wheeler was using binoculars to scan the country on the other side of the pass. Beside him Tabor stood like an aide to a general, quiet, respectful, ready to relay any orders the great man might decide to give.

Wheeler let the binoculars hang from his neck. "You know what I think?" he said to Tabor, who put on a trusted subordinate's face. "I think we've taught the bastards a lesson they'll never forget. Unless I'm wrong—and I always admit it— I'm convinced they'll think twice before they bother us again. What do you think, Mr. Tabor?"

Tabor knew how to kiss hind-end. "That could very well be," he weaseled. Then he brazened out his momentary embarrassment. "They'd have to be crazy, Mr. Wheeler. They lost nineteen men, sir. How many more can they afford to lose?"

Wheeler turned. "What do you think?" he said to Gatling. "Do you share Mr. Tabor's views?"

Wheeler was a capable engineer who had put the boots to his career. Had fucked himself—no one had to do it for him—

because of booze and ambition or greed, or because he had lost confidence in himself, and because of that important men had lost confidence in him. Gatling figured he'd never been the boy genius the newspapers said he was, but he must have been pretty good in his day. Which, at 40, was long in the past.

"Frobisher is being paid to stop you, kill you if he can," Gatling said. "He'll do it or die trying. If he doesn't, who else will give him an important job?"

That hit close to the bone, and Wheeler's face twisted in sudden anger. He tried to cover it by laughing. "Quite the doomsayer, aren't you? Haven't you ever been wrong?"

"Once or twice," Gatling said.

"Let's get the hell back to camp," Wheeler said.

"Well, he was a Marine, wasn't he?" Wheeler said with dull anger when Dr. LaPlante told him the wounded man had died in the late afternoon. He didn't want to hear about it, think about it. "A man has to take his chances when he enlists." Seeing the doctor's weary, disapproving expression, he tried to soften it a little. "Did he suffer much?"

Dr. LaPlante shrugged. "He just died, Mr. Wheeler."

Wheeler turned toward Irby, who had a drink ready. "He won't be forgotten, Doctor. We'll bury him like the hero he was."

It got dark. Guards were posted and food was sent up to them after it was cooked. Gatling sat with Mackenzie, drinking coffee. Mosquitoes ate at everybody. Sarah Morrison came over and Mackenzie said he had to check the guard.

"Anything interesting happen today?" Sarah Morrison asked, sounding listless. She sat down beside Gatling. "You know, I feel bad about that young man."

"Sure. Why not?"

"Well, I do. It's funny. You read about some battle where hundreds, thousands of men have been killed, and it doesn't mean anything. Then one young man dies and it all becomes reality."

"Sure. That's it. Reality."

"I'm too tired to be angry at you," she told him. "We had some times on the boat, didn't we?"

"Pretty good."

"I'm sorry I shut you out, Gatling. I felt stifled, sort of trapped, if you know what I mean."

"Sure," Gatling said. "It's not hard to figure."

"It shouldn't mean that we can't be friends?" She sounded as if she meant it.

Gatling wondered if she felt threatened. If so, she had good reason. Was she offering him a job? Her protector? She knew what he had done to Cleary's gunmen. Could it be she was looking at him in a different light? My hero!

"It was more comfortable on the ship," Gatling said.

"What?" Her face flushed. "Why do you say that? I didn't mean that. Why must you be so vulgar?"

The Marines were done eating and were getting as much sleep as the mosquitoes would allow. Mackenzie had taken Gatling's advice, had ordered them to smear mud on their faces. It smelled bad but it helped a little. And it would give them an advantage if they had to fight in the dark.

"Go shit in your hat," Gatling told Sarah Morrison.

"I suppose I deserve that," she said seriously. So goddamned serious tonight, Gatling thought. "I'm afraid, Gatling."

That was more like it. That was reality. Forget about the dead Marine. "You'll get over it," he said. "Back in New York you could get run over by a streetcar."

She tried to use her big green eyes on him, but it was too dark. So she used her voice, soft, husky, sincere. "I won't get over it," she murmured. "Can I sleep next to you tonight?"

Gatling didn't mind that one bit. It was better than sleeping next to a crocodile. "Sure thing," he told her. "But I have to stand my watch with the other men."

She took a silver flash from the side pocket of her linen coat and offered him a drink. It was real silver, must have cost a bundle.

"Too hot," he said.

"Not for me." She put the flask to her mouth and drank.

"Good," she said. "So good I'll have another."

Gatling watched her as she screwed the top back on the flask and put it away. Liquor was a great courage-giver, provided you got enough of it. But the fear came back when the liquor gave out, and then it was worse.

After two more drinks she whispered, "I wouldn't mind a little of what we did on the boat. What about you, pal?"

At any other time he would have jumped at the chance, but . . . well . . . this was different. There was a dead Marine under the lean-to, not that having a corpse around made that much difference. Gatling was thinking more of Frobisher, or El Tigre, or maybe a party of Indians with poisoned arrows. It would be a hell of a thing to be caught with his pants down.

"Please, dear," he said. "The neighbors will see us."

If a woman could flounce lying down, then she flounced. Turning over on her side, she dug him savagely with her elbow.

"You are a fucking coward," she said. A few minutes later she was asleep.

They buried the dead Marine—his name was Maddocks, a native of Dothan, Alabama—in the morning. Covered by Gatling's light gun, two of his friends dug the grave during the night. Gatling told them to dig it deep if they didn't want Maddocks to be dug up by jungle animals.

Wheeler delivered the eulogy, and it was a long one because he had put brandy in his breakfast coffee. He gave the dead man a number of new names: Mannix, McManus, Miller. Because the dead man was a Southerner, Wheeler found it necessary to hark back to the Civil War, the courage of Confederates, the "new" America where all men were once again united under one flag.

Finally he finished, and a corporal blew a bugle and they shoveled him under. Irby complimented Wheeler on his moving delivery. So did Tabor. But no one else.

They made good time to the top of the pass, with the Marines doing the donkey work, as usual. The country between the ruins and the pass had already been surveyed and mapped. About ten miles of jungle lay between the pass and the next stretch of mountains. A thick heat haze hung over the jungle, and the mountains in the distance looked vague and unsubstantial.

"Well, the map has a pass marked on it," Wheeler said, as if someone had challenged the pass's existence. "Damn rotten climate. Can't see it but it has to be there. The sooner we get started, the sooner we'll be there."

But it didn't turn out to be that easy. They came down from the pass into jungle so dense that machetes had to be used to chop a path through mile after mile of vines, creeping plants, and underbrush. The sky was overcast and the rain wasn't far off; under the trees that grew to great height the light was dark green, as if they were at the bottom of a scummy pond. Sweat ran off them like warm, sticky water; mosquitoes droned in, overpowering the stillness; and above all, it was hot.

Mackenzie's machete-wielders led the way, chopping and sweating. It was so hot and the work so hard they had to be relieved every hundred yards. One man collapsed, and he lay for a long time with his eyes rolled back in his head. Dr. Hazen said it was heat prostration. The Marine recovered in the hour it took for the civilians to catch up. After that, another man carried his carbine and machete and he walked like a man who had no idea where he was going.

At four o'clock in the afternoon Wheeler asked his head surveyor how far they'd come. The man said three miles from the bottom of the pass.

"Christ!" Wheeler said, sweat dripping from his chin. "I thought we did better than that."

"No, sir, Mr. Wheeler," the surveyor insisted. "Three miles. That's what the figures show."

Wheeler sent for Mackenzie, and told him to push his machete crews a little harder. "We have to find a halfway decent place to camp for the night. Tell them to put their backs into it."

For a moment Gatling thought Mackenzie was going to say something. But he didn't. All he did was nod and walk away.

They made camp in a place where the trees thinned out a bit. The Marines cleared the area of brush and vines while the tents were set up. Fritz and Irby set up Wheeler's tent while the great man watched. Mackenzie told his men to get a move on; it was going to rain. Nobody liked the sound of that because rain wouldn't cool off the terrible heat. If anything, it made it worse. It wouldn't even get rid of the mosquitoes.

Sick with heat and work, one Marine growled to another, "What a fucking place."

Mackenzie said, "Belay that talk, Zimmerman. Try to think of it as a summer vacation."

It looked like a small tent city by the time they got finished. The rain started as soon as supper was on the fire. The rain came straight down through the trees, heavy, steady, relentless, as if it meant to go on forever. Fires hissed out and half-cooked food was ruined. Wheeler's cook had started supper early, and the great man was the only one who could look forward to a decent supper. Tabor shared it with him, by invitation.

Rain or no rain, guards had to be posted. Night settled in and Gatling felt sorry for the poor sons of bitches that had to sit out there in the dark, in their dripping slickers. The heat was hard enough on a man in shirt and pants; under a slicker it was murderous. Gatling had two tents, one for himself, one for his weapons and ammunition. His tent wasn't so bad, he decided. It had a rubber groundsheet for a floor, and a folding canvas cot to sleep on, and the tent itself was new and well water-proofed. He'd been in worse fixes.

He lay on the cot in the dark, cleaning and oiling the light Maxim gun. The light gun came before anything else; this was his personal weapon; it had proved itself many times. No matter how many other weapons he tested for the Maxim Company, he always took the modified light gun along. It hadn't failed him yet.

He finished with the light gun, cased it, and put it under the cot. The case was lined with soft rubber to prevent the gun from being damaged. The rubber also kept it dry. Well, in most climates it would keep it dry, but here in steamy, stinking

Panama everything got wet. Everything got wet and everything rotted; he knew he had his work cut out for him.

He was working on the Mondragon automatic rifle when Sarah Morrison came to his tent. By now he was so familiar with the weapon that he could work on it in the dark. He knew she was headed his way because he heard her swearing as she stumbled through the mud. She sounded drunk or close to it.

"What the hell are you doing?" she said when she raised the tent flap and stooped to come in. "Why don't you have a light, for Christ's sake?"

Gatling told her what he was doing. "I don't need a light."

"Wheeler has a light." She sat down on the edge of the cot and he smelled the brandy she'd been drinking. A young lady with money, she drank good stuff.

"Why does Wheeler have a light and you don't?"

"A light makes too good a target," Gatling told her. "If Wheeler wants to risk it, that's his business. If they come, they'll shoot at a light before anything else."

Gatling cased the rifle and put it with the light Maxim. She stretched out beside him, hot and restless. "What's all this talk about light? What do we need a light for?"

"Not a thing," Gatling said.

Later, after taking a look around, he came back and saw that she had gone back to her tent.

They stayed under canvas for five days, the length of time it took the rain to stop. Even in the rain they could have moved on, but Wheeler was reluctant to do it, so they stayed. Two Marines and three of Wheeler's men came down with fever; when that happened there was no question of going anywhere. The stricken men would die or get well, but they couldn't be moved in the rain. It took the doctors two days to agree that the five men had yellow fever. The diagnosis was a death sentence; all they could do was wait for the five men to die.

They didn't die easy, and while the rain came down, the five patients, now housed in two tents, raved and screamed all day and all night. Nobody was allowed near the patients—not that anybody tried. Fear was in everyone's eyes, and Gatling knew they were all thinking the same thing. Do I have it? Am I going to get it?

Only O'Sullivan didn't seem to give a damn; he was the only one who remained cheerful. He stayed in his tent, with his cameras and photographic plates laid out on his cot. Sometimes he whistled. This grated on everyone's nerves, even Gatling's. Gatling liked O'Sullivan, but found his ghoulishness a bit hard to take.

"Well, what do you want me to do? Cry in my beer?" he said when Gatling told him to stop the goddamned whistling. "I mean no disrespect by it. Those poor devils can't hear me."

"The rest of the camp can hear you. It's getting on their nerves."

O'Sullivan stuck a cigar in his mouth and put a match to it. "Why are they so afraid of death? It's the most natural thing in the world."

O'Sullivan could be an exasperating fellow. Gatling said, "Everybody knows that, Tim, but most people try to put it off as long as possible."

O'Sullivan blew smoke, enjoying his illicit cigar. "Gatling," he said, "Leaving the dying men out of it, there's some alive tonight that'll be under the sod not long from now. I know the signs, and I don't mean thee or me."

"Stupid Irish superstition," Sarah Morrison snapped when Gatling told her about it. "Tim may be a fine photographer, but at heart he's just a superstitious mick. He knows the signs! What signs? Did he tell you?"

They were in Gatling's tent, eating canned beef and drinking coffee. The rain drummed down with relentless force, turning the rain forest into a swamp. Two of the men had died; the others were close to it. It was steaming hot in the tent, but Sarah Morrison shivered.

"I didn't ask him about the signs," Gatling said. "His sign talk may be bullshit, but he's right. Some of us are going to die. You asked me, so I'm telling you."

"Jesus Christ! How I'd like to be back in New York. In City Hall Park, right across from Park Row, where the *World* is, people are sitting on benches, reading newspapers, feeding the pigeons. That's what I'd like to be doing. What I mean is, I'd like to be in Rector's eating my lunch." Sarah Morrison poked at the canned beef on her plate. "This stuff is shit."

Gatling continued to eat. He had eaten canned beef in various parts of the world and it always tasted the same—lousy. The coffee was bad, but he drank it. He wasn't fussy about food. What he'd like most, he decided, was a cold mug of beer.

"You'll be back," he said.

"You're sure of that?"

"You bet I am."

"Yes, but do you swear it?" she wanted to know.

"On a stack of bibles," Gatling answered. What was the use of panicking the girl?

Chapter
SIX

The last man died on the day the rain stopped. They buried him and moved on. He died early in the morning, so they had a whole day ahead of them. Wheeler delivered no more eulogies; what praying there was was done by Mackenzie, who kept it short.

As the cloud cover lifted, so did everyone's spirits. No one else had come down with fever. Their progress was slow, the engineers and surveyors were working again, but no one complained. They had survived, and for the moment that was enough.

Because the jungle was flat and the trees grew high, they couldn't see the mountains. Wheeler fretted about the pass when he was sober. Was it there or wasn't it?

No one could give him an answer, but his head engineer said, "The first pass was there, Mr. Wheeler. Why wouldn't the other one be?"

Wheeler clapped the engineer on the shoulder. "You're right, Mr. Garth. Of course you're right. Why wouldn't it be?"

Travel got easier as they got closer to the mountains; Mackenzie's men didn't have to swing machetes from dawn till dusk. At night, in spite of the heat and the mosquitoes, there was a better feeling in camp. One night, boisterous with brandy,

Wheeler congratulated everybody on the fine job they were doing. They were the salt of the earth, the finest bunch he'd worked with in his entire life.

"You can tell your grandchildren . . ." He went on and on, pausing only when he knew they wanted to applaud.

"It won't last," O'Sullivan said ominously. "It can't last. All the odds are against it."

Gatling told him to go shit in his hat; Sarah Morrison's remark had become a joke between them. But he knew the Irishman was right. Six men were dead, and that was just a beginning.

One morning they walked out of the jungle into a long stretch of open country that sloped up into the mountains. It was covered with scrub and dotted with rocks, but they could see the mountains and the sky. The heat was fierce but bearable, nothing like it had been in the jungle.

They had stopped to rest. Wheeler had unslung his binoculars, and was scanning the point in the mountains where the pass should be. "I don't know," he said. "It's there, but it doesn't look right. It looks like it's blocked. How does it look to you, Mr. Garth?"

The head engineer talked while he used his binoculars. "There's a pass there, or there was. You're right, Mr. Wheeler. Something isn't right up there. We have to get closer."

Wheeler took another look. "A rock slide, you think?"

Garth said, "I'm afraid it's more than that. More like the whole side of the mountain has fallen in on it. Mr. Wheeler, we have to go up there. No other way to be sure."

"What the hell are we waiting for?" Wheeler said. "Let's get up there and look at the bastard. Everybody up! Everybody move!"

Wheeler was already on his way by the time everything— tents, boxes, crates, rubber boats, surveying instruments, rods and chains—were picked up and carried. Wheeler didn't have to carry anything but himself. In the rough places he hurried, in the smooth places he ran. Mackenzie told Tabor to stay with the supplies. Tabor was glad to do it.

Gatling and Mackenzie went up the long slope after Wheeler.

Irby was with Wheeler, looking worried, telling him to slow down. "Easy, Dock. Go easy, Dock,' Irby kept repeating, but Wheeler didn't hear him or wouldn't listen. Wheeler was only 40, but booze and high living had taken their toll. He gasped. He sweated like a pig. Keeping up with Gatling without effort, Mackenzie smiled, and Gatling could have sworn that the Scotsman touched his finger to his temple—the loony sign. Or maybe he was just scratching at a mosquito bite.

Wheeler was exhausted when they got to the foot of the pass. He staggered to a halt, shaded his eyes with his hand, and looked up. Then he seemed to remember he had a pair of binoculars, and he used them, moving them this way and that.

What he saw made him curse. "Fuck it!" he roared. "Godddamn and fuck it! It's not there! The fucking thing isn't there. It was there, but it's not there now. Gone, buried. The fucking thing is buried."

"Easy does it, Dock," Irby said. "Take it easy."

Wheeler shoved Irby and he fell. "Get away from me," Wheeler roared. He turned to Mackenzie, wild-eyed. "Where's Mr. Garth?"

"Right here, Mr. Wheeler," Garth said, coming up the slope. Garth was a calm, steady man, older than the other engineers. Gatling could see why Wheeler depended on Garth. He had a slight Scots-Canadian accent. He didn't panic.

"Aye," he said after using his binoculars. "The whole side of the mountain has fallen down on it. We'll never get over that, sir. No way, Mr. Wheeler. It's three hundred feet high. Must have been an earth tremor that caused it. But not lately. Look, Mr. Wheeler, here and here. It must have happened a long time ago."

Wheeler sat down on a rock. "God damn that goddamned map!"

Garth said, "It's a very old map, Mr. Wheeler. A copy of a very old map. Accurate enough in its time, I'd say, but . . ."

Irby was up on his feet, dusting off his clothes. He wasn't hurt, but his feelings were. Gatling and Mackenzie just stood there. It was all between Wheeler and his chief engineer.

Wheeler slumped in dejection. "What's to be done, Mr. Garth? We can't climb over it?"

Garth looked up at what had once been a narrow gap in the mountains. "No sir," he said calmly. "We can't climb over that. Even without the gear, the supplies, we couldn't climb over that. A mountain climber could, probably, but not us."

Wheeler looked up. He had been staring at the ground. "What's to be done, Mr. Garth?" he said again.

Gatling decided that Garth was the only friend Wheeler had in the entire outfit. Or maybe he wasn't. It was hard to say what he was. Whatever he was, he was good at his job.

"We'll have to go south and go around," Garth said. "Then come north again, along the far side of the mountain, till we're right opposite where we are now."

Wheeler looked up at the mountain as if he hated it. Maybe he did. Gatling could see why he might. He didn't know many geologists or engineers, men who might hate mountains.

"Where we are, Mr. Garth," Wheeler said, "is nowhere. But stand by, will you? I have to think. Where's Irb?"

Irby stepped in with a liquor flask he took from his pocket. "I think you need a drink, Dock. Anybody would."

Wheeler took the flask and drank from it. He drank two more long drinks before he gave it back. "Thank you, Irb. Sorry I pushed you. An accident."

Irby put the flask back in his pocket. "Actually, I tripped."

Gatling wondered how much Irby had to do with Wheeler's drinking. Maybe nothing. Maybe everything. Something about the two men wasn't right. He seemed to remember that Wheeler had a wife somewhere.

"You're right, Mr. Garth," Wheeler said, as the liquor took effect. "We'll go around the goddamned fucking mountain and take up where we left off. The good old Monkey River cuts through the mountains. We'll follow the good old Monkey River through the mountains, then head back north. Only trouble, Mr. Garth, is this. Goddamned wild Indians live along the good old Monkey River, or so they tell me."

Wheeler turned to look at Gatling. "Is that what they tell you, Mr. Gatling? All kind of wild Panama Indians along the Monkey River? Poisoned arrows, cannibals, beautiful wild Indian maidens looking to be jabbed by the hundred-percent-American white man?"

"All I heard is the part about the poisoned arrows," Gatling said.

"Cupid's arrows are far more dangerous," Wheeler said, looking at Irby. Irby looked away. Wheeler got the flask back and drank it empty. "But let's not worry too much about arrows of any kind. They'll get a great big surprise if they attack us. Isn't that right, Mr. Gatling?"

"That's the idea," Gatling agreed.

They went south, skirting the edge of the mountains, moving away from them when they had to. At times they came to places that looked like the beginning of another pass. Wheeler got excited every time they saw one; a lot of time was wasted exploring dead ends. Finally even Wheeler became convinced that the mountains here couldn't be crossed.

Most members of the party seemed to have adopted the idea that they would deal with the Mono River and its Indians when the time came. For now, they were glad to be out of the jungle. Another idea passed around was that it was healthier where they were now. Gatling didn't know whether this was true. At least it was possible to breathe without feeling suffocated. One of the worst things about the jungle was the sick-sweet stink in the air, the ever-present awareness of decay. The stink was worse in some places than in others. One way or another, it was always there.

It was a good 15 miles to the river, no great distance in open country, even with all the supplies and equipment they had to carry. Moving along the base of the mountains, blocked here and there by enormous rockfalls, forced to rest because of the terrible heat, they had come no more than seven miles by the end of the day. But they were out of the jungle; that was the main thing; no one wanted to think beyond the here and now. The next day would come.

That night camp was a wide, flat place with rocks on all sides. It was high up, a sort of shelf cut into the side of the mountain. A lot of it was covered with shale, but there was enough soft ground to set up the tents. Under canvas the heat was bad, even at night, but a tent did offer some protection from the mosquitoes. Besides, there was always the chance of more rain. After looking at the evening sky Gatling didn't think it would rain, but that was just a guess. In some other places, in country he knew well, he could be fairly sure he was right. Not here, though: Panama was full of surprises.

He studied their position while the light lasted. As good as they were likely to find, he decided. No chance of attack from above. Nothing but a bird or a mountain goat could get up there. A shaley, crumbling slope went down from their camp. Anybody trying to climb it after dark would find it rough going. It could be done—but not without making a lot of noise. The camp could be defended, though not for any great length of time, but long enough to give them a chance.

As long as it didn't rain, they could stay outdoors until it was time to sleep. Up high, the air was better in spite of the heat; there was no longer the feeling of being buried alive. That, more than anything, made them feel better. Gatling hoped they wouldn't fall apart when real trouble came.

It hadn't come yet. The killing of Cleary's ambushers was no great victory. Gatling knew that better than the others; at least better than the civilians. If Cleary had posted men to watch his back, it wouldn't have happened at all. Cleary was just a gunman. Frobisher would be different; a capable officer by all accounts. No matter that he was a killer. A lot of officers were killers.

Gatling tried to get a picture of Frobisher in his mind, but there wasn't much to go on. All he had were the bare bones of the man's life. Cashiered officer. Strikebreaker. Gunrunner. Mercenary. A man with a cruel, violent nature who killed for a living. Nothing new about any of it.

What Frobisher would do could only be guessed at. No way to be sure about what he knew about the Maxim Company's weapons: the light gun, the automatic rifle, the mortar, the new explosive. Gatling figured he knew *something*. The men who wanted to destroy the expedition had their spies, the colonel said. There might even be a spy on the colonel's payroll, somebody who provided information for a price.

If Frobisher knew about the weapons, he might hang back and try to wear them down, not a hard thing to do in country like this. Gatling had been through it, knew what it was like. During his early cavalry days he was attached to an infantry regiment in the Black Hills. Most of the Sioux had been driven out, but a number of war parties remained. One war party, led by a half-breed called Running Wolf, gave them the most trouble. Day after day they sniped from the high ground, killing men and horses. They picked their targets and seldom missed. They never made a fight of it. They sniped and ran, disappearing into the hills they knew so well and the soldiers not at all. If Running Wolf hadn't been betrayed by a subchief who hated him, his small war of attribution could have dragged on for months.

Frobisher could do it like that. Men who could fight with the best of them could have their nerves worn down by the unexpected. It was not knowing that got to them; in the Black Hills he had seen men twitch with fear when a teamster cracked his whip, and these men were seasoned soldiers, not civilians a few years out of college.

Hit and run. That was the way to do it. Gatling knew that was the way he would do it. Wear the enemy down until he's ready to jump out of his skin, then attack full force. Deliver a hammer blow when he's at his weakest. Get it over in a hurry.

Gatling knew the civilians would go to pieces if it went on too long. A few might not. All they had were revolvers, but even if they were better armed, what good would rifles be against an unseen enemy?

A rifle cracked, a man died. That might be the only shot fired that day. Or it could go on from sunup to sundown. At night they could snipe at the guards, or just shoot into the darkened camp to keep everyone awake . . . .

Thinking of the sleep he might not get, Gatling turned in for the night. Mackenzie insisted on it. ''If we need you, we know where to find you,'' Mackenzie said.

During the night Sarah Morrison came to his tent. By then he'd had all the sleep he needed, and they wrestled until dawn. Drinking coffee while the sun came up, Sarah Morrison said, ''I think I know what I'm going to order at Rector's. . . .''

They saw the Mono River before they reached it. It flowed through a wide gap in the mountains, spreading out to form vast swamps many miles across. Flooding had followed five days of rain. In the morning it was shrouded by twisting fog that from a distance looked like smoke. The sun burned off the fog, but it came back at night. And even by day the Mono River country was sinister and forbidding. The swamps steamed and bubbled, and crocodiles slithered through the mud.

''May not be as bad as it looks,'' the head engineer told Wheeler. ''We'll follow along the edge of the river till we get through the mountains. The floods, though, are a problem. No doubt about it. Mr. Wheeler, you want to camp a few days, wait for the water level to go down?''

Wheeler looked dejected. ''I have to think about it, Mr. Garth.''

They were having a conference outside Wheeler's big tent. It was late in the afternoon. There was daylight left, but the river and the flooded swamp were less than two miles away.

Wheeler always asked for advice when he was unsure of himself, and that usually happened when he was sober. Wheeler sober meant hung over; there was no day when he was free of alcohol. He got up needing a drink; that night he fell asleep drunk. That was his routine, and it didn't change from one day to another. If there hadn't been danger, his drinking wouldn't have mattered so much. His subordinates could have done the work without him. The trouble with Wheeler was, he liked to

stick his nose into everything when he had a snootful. He could
be a bully when he felt like it. Sometimes he changed things
that didn't need changing.

The rest of them waited while Wheeler thought important
thoughts. Finally he looked up and said they would go on in
the morning. "The water level may not go down for a week.
If it rains before then, the floods will be worse. We'll follow
the river, keeping to the high ground. Mr. Mackenzie, send
some men down there to see what it's like. Tell them to scout
along the river a mile or so. That should give us some idea what
to expect."

That sounded sensible enough. "First thing in the morning,
sir," Mackenzie said.

Wheeler glared at him. "Send them *now*."

Mackenzie was angry enough to argue about it. "But it'll be
full dark by the time they reach the river. It's too dangerous
to go in there in the dark."

"Send them. That's an order." Wheeler went into his tent,
dropping the flap behind him. The meeting broke up. Mackenzie
walked away and Gatling followed him. It was the first time
Gatling had seen him so mad.

"Take it easy," Gatling told him. "That son of a bitch could
do a lot of harm. Back home, I mean."

Mackenzie ground his hands together. "If we ever get there.
What the hell harm can he do to me? I'm ready to call it quits
right now. The Corps is in a sorry state when it puts men under
the command of a drunken jackass like that. Politics!
Goddamned politics! You can get away with anything if you
have the right connections."

"Simmer down," Gatling said. "You don't want to wreck
your career. You know Tabor doesn't like you. He'd jump at
the chance to nail you up."

Mackenzie's face was grim. "You got that right, Mr. Gatling.
I'm not his class, you see. Not a gentleman. A jumped-up
enlisted man."

Gatling pushed it: He didn't want to see Mackenzie busted
out of the Marines after 25 years' honorable service.

"Don't let him do it, Mr. Mackenzie," Gatling said.

"Ah, for Christ's sake, what's all this *mister* shit? Call me Mac. You don't seem to mind Gatling."

"It'll do. Have you been listening, Mac? I don't usually give advice. Watch out for Tabor and Irby. They'll do you dirt. Tabor because he's ambitious and doesn't like you. Irby will do anything Wheeler tells him to do."

"Irby's a dirty little queer," Mackenzie said, still angry but calming down. "I don't know what Wheeler is. What the hell do I care what they are. Just as long as they don't come after me."

"You're too ugly."

"You're no beauty yourself."

"Then it's all right?" Gatling said. "You're not going to do anything dumb? Like punch Wheeler in the mouth?"

"Lord, but wouldn't I like to," Mackenzie said. "No, I'll do as he says, but I'll go down there with my men. Make sure they don't drown or get sucked under. But should that happen, Wheeler will get more than a smack in the mouth."

Gatling watched them going down the long slope in the red light of the setting sun. Everything, mountain and jungle, was red at that time of day. Except for the noise coming from Wheeler's tent, it was very quiet on the side of the mountain. Politics, Gatling thought. Goddamned politics! Mackenzie and his men were risking their lives in a dark, stinking swamp while the great man and his friends drank aged brandy and congratulated themselves on how successful they were.

It was a hell of a way to run an expedition.

Chapter
SEVEN

"There's a lot of crocs and snakes in there," Mackenzie said. "So we'll have to watch ourselves. Flood has disturbed the creatures and they're all over the place. Last night we came close to walking into a nest of snakes. O'Hara got struck in the boot. The fangs didn't penetrate. The luck of the Irish."

Still spattered with mud, Mackenzie stood beside Wheeler on firm ground at the edge of the swamp. A few hours earlier, Wheeler had lurched out of his tent with the anguish of a bad hangover in his bloodshot eyes. Somewhat subdued, it was still there. Behind him, civilians and Marines were ready to go.

Sweat ran down the sides of Wheeler's lardy, handsome face. "How far upriver did you go?"

"About two miles, sir. That's what you said. Should be possible to get through. Possible but very difficult. Some firm ground does verge on the floodwater. In places, that is. Other places it's all swamp."

Wheeler grunted. "You went two miles? You can't say what it's like past that point?"

"No, sir," Mackenzie said. "It could be better—or worse. We're ready, sir."

"Of course you're ready. I told you to be ready. Get a move on, mister. We haven't got all day." Wheeler turned to Irby, who handed him a canteen. In his tent he drank from the cap of his hammered-silver liquor flask. On the march he drank from a canteen like the rest of the fellows. The difference was, Wheeler had brandy in his water.

A hot wind came through the gap in the mountains, ruffling the dark water of the river, but doing nothing to lessen the skull-popping heat. The sun beat down like a hammer on an anvil. Mud sucked at their boots as they started into the river gap. On both sides of the river and the swamp the mountains climbed up to more than a thousand feet. High up, black smudges in a blue sky, buzzards circled lazily, gliding down on the hot wind, ravenous but wary.

They came to a place where part of the rock wall had collapsed. It was a good place to rest because the rock was dry and out of the water. But getting the equipment and supplies across took some doing. Gatling stayed close to the boxes and cases that contained his weapons and ammunition. The Marines sweated like pigs before they got everything up and over.

"I feel like my feet're going to rot off," one Marine said to another.

"How could you tell the difference?" his friend said. "You always did have smelly feet."

Nobody had dry feet, not even Wheeler, and he had glazed rubber boots up past his knees. Water seeped in, and so did bad-smelling mud. The mud stank like an open sewer under the noon day sun. Ahead of them crocodiles slid into the water. So far none of the monsters had attacked, but Mackenzie told his men to keep their carbines ready. More dangerous than the crocodiles were the snakes. Panama was infested with snakes, most of them poisonous.

It wasn't all bad, just most of it. There were stretches of firm ground smack up against the river canyon wall. There they made pretty good time, grateful for being able to walk without black muck sucking at their boots. The mud was a terrible strain on the legs; it was like walking in diver's boots. The Marines suffered more than the others because of all they had to carry. Shamed into helping out, the civilians didn't do near as well:

They weren't used to donkey work.

The worst scare they had was in the late afternoon, when a huge crocodile came gliding right at them. Sarah Morrison screamed and tried to run. There was nowhere to run to. The Marines with rifles opened fire, but the croc kept coming. Gunfire echoed between the towering rock walls, and it sounded like everybody was yelling at the same time. The croc came roaring out of the water, its awful mouth yawning, very fast on its stumpy legs. Mackenzie stepped forward and shot the monster in the eye. The croc roared and died and slid back into the water. The carcass floated away with other crocs tearing at it.

Mackenzie grinned at Gatling. "The garden spot of the world," he said, pushing the empty shell from the cylinder. He loaded a bullet, pushed the loading gate back in place, and holstered his revolver.

Bateman Olds looked at Mackenzie, and wrote something in his leather-covered notebook. Wheeler, after a long drink from his canteen, clapped Mackenzie on the shoulder and told him he was one hell of a fellow. Tabor looked jealous.

The rock walls fell away, and the river widened out into a lake with small green islands in it. On Wheeler's map it was marked as *lago de los indios*—Lake of the Indians, in English.

"Well, by God, it's there all right," Wheeler said, slurring his words a little. "But where are the goddamned *indios*?"

"It's a copy of a very old map," Irby said. "The Indians probably died out years ago."

Wheeler swigged from the canteen, then shook it. "Poor indios. But not poor me. I'm not poor, Irb."

Irby smiled.

They made camp on a pebbly beach as far back from the lake as they could get. Crocodiles were still a threat, especially after it got dark. The Marines groaned as they laid down their burdens. Sarah Morrison always needed help to set up her tent. Usually the civilians fell over their feet in their eagerness to be of service. Tonight they were sullen and tired. Gatling helped her instead.

Fires were started, guards were posted, and night settled down over the lake. Fish jumped in the water. Crocodiles glided in the dark water, but didn't crawl up on the beach because they were afraid of fires. Having fires was risky—they could be seen for miles—but here they were necessary because of the crocs.

Gatling took the light gun from its case and set it up in his tent. Two belts of 600 rounds were in the metal ammunition box clipped to the side of the gun and level with the cartridge feed. The light gun was ready to kill the moment he fired the activating shot. He checked the Maximite sticks, the cigar, and the matches in his pocket. An airtight case kept the matches dry. The cigar would draw all right if he had to light it. He checked the loads in the Colt. He checked the automatic rifle. Satisfied that everything was in working order, he stretched out on the cot and slept.

He woke when he thought he heard something. His watch said it was five minutes to two. He pulled back the tent flap and went outside with the Colt in his hand. The lake was washed in pale yellow moonlight; there wasn't a sound except for water washing up on the beach. The Marine guard closest to his tent still sat with his back against a rock. He saw the man's shape, the carbine cradled in his arms. I'm getting as jumpy as the rest of them, he thought.

He got back on the cot and tried to get back to sleep. An instant later a man screamed. Gatling picked up the light gun and went outside. Jesus! A whole fleet of dugout canoes was coming in toward the beach. Indians were jumping into shallow water as the dugouts grated on banked pebbles. Other Indians were already ashore. They were screaming now, and running fast, their bodies and faces smeared with bright colors. Gatling put the light gun against his hip and opened fire. He moved forward as he fired, swinging the barrel of the light gun from right to left. He chopped them down as they charged up the beach in wave after wave. Bodies piled up. They kept coming. Their spears had metal tips, were decorated with feathers. They didn't throw the spears. They ran forward with the spears, using them like bayonets. He didn't know how many there were, maybe hundreds. He didn't know how many he'd killed and kept on killing. Mackenzie's men were firing steadily, firing and loading, firing and reloading. Screams and shouts, the crash of carbines, the crack-crack of pistols echoed out across the lake. The light gun chattered in Gatling's hand, and more and more savages went down. The shore of the lake blazed with gunfire. He wondered how Sarah Morrison was doing with her .38. He hoped she was firing it and not running half-crazy in the dark. He hoped she wasn't dead. . . .

He got a tighter hold on the light gun and forced himself to fire shorter bursts. His hands were slick with sweat. He swung the gun around and cut down a bunch of them coming at him from behind. They died kicking and howling, sounding more like animals than men. They were animals, but he didn't hate them. How could you hate animals? He just wanted to kill them before they killed him. And then he heard what he thought of as the *sound,* the change of pitch that comes in every battle. He had heard it before. There was always that sound when one side started to lose. They were pulling back. Trying to pull back. They were pushing dugouts into the water, hanging onto the sides. Some of them lost their hold and sank when the canoes hit deep water. The beach was littered with dead. He had to climb over dead bodies to get to the water's edge. The moon was clouding over; they were vanishing into darkness. He kept on firing until his bullets ran out. Out on the dark lake there wasn't a sound.

He walked back up from the beach and found Mackenzie bent over a dead Marine. A feathered arrow stuck out of his shoulder. Mackenzie pulled it out and looked at the tip. The metal tip had grooves in it.

"Careful with that," Gatling warned. Mackenzie's right hand was bleeding from a cut. "It's got poison on it. He wouldn't be dead if it wasn't poisoned."

"Dear Lord!" Mackenzie was appalled. "To die like that! The filthy, murdering savages. I was asleep. I woke up. I thought I was having a nightmare."

Mackenzie put the dead Marine's hat on his face. "Nothing

we can do for this poor fellow. I hate to think what we're going to find.''

''Some of our people have to be dead,'' Gatling told him. ''It just depends how many.''

They left the dead Marine and went up to where the tents were. Mackenzie got his Marines lined up. Three dead, one wounded. Two of the dead had been killed by poisoned arrows. The third dead man had taken a spear thrust through his guts. ''I'm not going to die, am I?'' the wounded man asked Mackenzie. ''I saw the other men when the arrows hit. A minute later they dropped dead. I just got stabbed by a spear. It's only a deep cut in my arm.''

Mackenzie told him to report to the doctor. ''Dr. Hazen is dead,'' the Marine said. ''I saw him get hit. An arrow. Jesus! The look on his face. I think Dr. LaPlante is all right.''

Mackenzie lost his temper. ''Then report to him, you idiot. On the double. Get the hell away from me.'' He turned to Gatling. ''This is a terrible thing to happen. What the hell are we doing here anyway?''

''Making maps, I guess. It's nobody's fault. You can't even blame Wheeler for it. We had to camp where we did.''

Shillitoe and three civilians had been killed, struck down by poisoned arrows. A surveyor with a gaping spear wound in his abdomen was dying. Dr. LaPlante said bitterly, ''I really don't have that much work to do,'' meaning that once a man was struck by a poisoned arrow he could be regarded as dead.

Sarah Morrison was talking to Olds, who had his notebook in one hand, a fountain pen in the other. Whatever she was saying, Olds kept nodding.

Wheeler, Irby, and Tabor had survived. O'Sulllivan, with not a scratch on him, was taking nighttime photographs with magnesium flares. Mackenzie warned him to keep away from the dead Marines or he'd throw him to the crocs. Out in the lake the crocodiles were feasting on dead Indians.

''Listen to Mr. Mackenzie, Tim,'' Gatling said.

O'Sullivan shrugged and walked away, followed by his

assistant. Soon they were photographing dead Indians. The flares
were like silent explosions in the darkness.

Mackenzie reported to Wheeler, told him how many men the
Indians had killed. "Four of your people." He gave their names.
"Mr. Simms will die. Three of my men are dead. One is
wounded, but he'll probably recover. Dr. Hazen is dead."

Wheeler's normally ruddy face had turned a sickly color. His
mouth twitched. "That many," he said.

Mackenzie's face had no expression on it. "If we count Mr.
Simms as dead, we have lost fourteen men since the start of
this expedition."

Wheeler was glad to have somebody to attack. "Damn it,
mister! Damn your impudence! Don't you think I can count?
Answer me."

Gatling, standing by, could feel the tension in Mackenzie's
wiry body.

"I know you can count, sir," Mackenzie said. "I was simply
making an observation. Nothing more than that."

Wheeler drank from his expensive flask. As a rule, he did
his flask drinking in his tent. Gatling didn't think Wheeler was
a brutal man at heart. The booze had done him in. The booze
and maybe Irby. Just the same, there was no call to humiliate
Mackenzie in front of the others. Especially in front of a fellow
officer. Gatling felt like taking the booze flask and shoving it
down his throat.

"Keep your observations to yourself, Mackenzie." Wheeler
tried to calm his twanging nerves with another drink. "You're
not being paid to make observations. Is that clear?"

"Quite clear, sir."

"Carry on then," Wheeler said, trying to sound like a soldier.
Then he raised his voice and called after Mackenzie. "Throw
those filthy Indian savages in the lake. See to it personally. But
get it done."

Dumping the Indians bodies in the lake was a mistake.
Crocodiles came gliding from all over the lake, drawn by the
smell of blood. The noise was hideous. Sleep was impossible.

All night long the crocodiles fought and roared, driven crazy by so much human flesh. Gatling lay in his cot and decided the crocs sounded like politicians at the pork barrel.

During the night he had visitors; they all said they couldn't sleep. He could have slept if he felt the need of it, but he didn't. Besides, there were still some hours of darkness left; anything could happen before morning.

O'Sullivan came first, like a man out for a stroll in the cool of the evening. In the tent it was at least a hundred degrees, and O'Sullivan's cigar didn't make the muggy air any better. Gatling had a folding stool with a canvas seat, and O'Sullivan sat on it. Nothing about him suggested that he'd just been photographing dead savages.

"Well, it's not such a bad night," O'Sullivan started off.

Gatling lay with his hands behind his head. "I'm glad you think so, Tim. You like this kind of climate, do you?"

O'Sullivan smoked his cheap cigar like a banker enjoying an after dinner Romeo Y Julieta. "Heat doesn't bother me all that much. I'm so thin there's not a lot to sweat out." He raised the tent flap and flicked cigar ashes outside. "Lord, but you killed a power of aborigines tonight."

The Irishman worked every conversation around to his favorite subject—death. Gatling wondered if the Civil War hadn't made him a little crazy.

"I didn't see you do any shooting," Gatling said.

"What good would a gun do me? I couldn't hit Senator Church at ten paces." Senator Church was a grossly fat politician. "One time I tried my hand at a shooting gallery in Coney Island. You know what happened?"

"What?"

"I shot the poor feller behind the counter. Oh, he didn't die or anything like that, but it put me off guns for life."

"You don't say?"

"I do say." O'Sullivan gave Gatling a sly look. He was a born gossip. It was part of his malicious nature. "What do you think of that little dust-up between Wheeler and Mr. Mackenzie? You was dere, as they say in the Five Points."

Gatling looked at the V roof of the tent. O'Sullivan was like the colonel. You had to take him in small doses.

"Wheeler is a jackass," Gatling said.

"A jackass with a loud bray. He may be on the skids, but he can slip poor old Mackenzie a mickey any time he chooses."

O'Sullivan had spent a lot of time in McGurk's Suicide Palace on the Bowery. It got its name from the many down-and-out streetwalkers who killed themselves in the balcony. Most of them drank vitriol. O'Sullivan liked to tell stories about it. He had picked up the lingo.

"He'll forget about Mackenzie," Gatling said. "He wouldn't take the time to nail up a lowly lieutenant."

"Tabor won't forget." O'Sullivan seemed sure of what he was saying. "Tabor is a vicious little turd. I think he hates Mackenzie because Mackenzie is a man and he isn't even half a man."

O'Sullivan was about to go on about Tabor, but Gatling had heard enough bullshit for one night. "Look, Tim, you let Mackenzie worry about Tabor if he's so inclined. Now get the hell out of here."

"I can take a hint," O'Sullivan said.

Gatling's next visitor was a young engineer named Jones. He hadn't spoken to the man since they'd been introduced the night of the drunken shipboard party in Brooklyn. He was quiet, serious-looking—and come to think of it, he hadn't been drunk that night. He was in his middle twenties, somewhere in there, and he had thinning hair and startled eyes. That was just the way his eyes looked, Gatling knew.

"I know it's late," he said apologetically. "But I have to talk to you. All right if I sit down?"

Gatling nodded. If anyone else came to his tent, he would have to charge admission. Now he knew how clergymen felt when people came to bare their souls. Father Gatling.

"If you say no, we won't hold it against you," Jones said. "But we urge you, the other fellows and I, to give it every consideration."

Gatling said, "I'll consider it if you tell me what it is. Keep it short. I know it's confidential. Go ahead.''

Jones took a deep breath. ''As you know, this expedition is
a mess. It was poorly planned, it's going badly, it'll be a miracle
if any of us survive. It's not all Mr. Wheeler's fault—the disease,
the awful climate. Obviously . . . The thing is, we look to him
for leadership, but it just isn't there. He drinks too much, he
makes wrong decisions, he doesn't seem to know what he's
doing. It has to get worse . . . . Mr. Gatling, we want to quit.''

''Then quit. You're all civilians. He can't make you stay.
The hell with your contracts. Let him sue you. He won't.
Depend on that. Go on home.'' That's what Gatling said, but
he knew it wasn't that simple.

Jones said, ''I wish we could just walk out and go home like
you say. But how are we to do it? What if those savages come after
us? We didn't kill all of them. Maybe they'll raise every Indian
between here and the sea. What about the gunmen, the
mercenaries? This Frobisher? And the rebels? We're no match
for men like that. All we have are revolvers. Eight of our people
are dead.''

Gatling wanted to get some sleep before morning. ''What do
you want me to do? Say it plain.''

Another deep breath. Jones said quickly, ''We want you to
take us out, Mr. Gatling. Get us safe to Panama City. You
. . . you and your weapons are our only chance of getting out
alive. Will you do it? We'll pay you anything you ask. Some
of the men have wealthy families. They'll be glad to pay. We
don't mean to insult you, sir.''

''I'm not insulted,'' Gatling said, thinking it was hard to insult
him when it came to money. He needed all the money he could
get for his Zunis. The war with the Copper Trust land-grabbers
and their hired Apaches had left the tribe in bad shape. He owed
them more than he could ever repay. He would send them money
as long as they needed it.

''I can't do it,'' Gatling said. ''I've already been paid. I can't
go back on it. I'd be finished if I did. Didn't you know anything
about Wheeler before you came to work for him?''

''We didn't know a thing, Mr. Gatling.'' Gatling wasn't sure

Jones was telling the truth. "It looked like a great opportunity, a big chance to get started. Working with Mr. Wheeler . . . Mr. Gatling, we'll pay double what you're getting now."

Gatling held onto his temper. "I don't want your money. I won't do it. Does Garth know about this?"

"No. We know Garth wouldn't do it. Garth has been with Wheeler a long time."

"All right," Gatling said. "Here's my advice. Take it or leave it. Stay with the outfit and you'll have a better chance. Go off on your own and you're done for. Frobisher won't know and won't care that you're no longer working for Wheeler. He'll kill you because it's part of the job. The rebels, if you run into them, will kill you for your boots, never mind the side arms. Your choice, Jones. What's it going to be?"

Jones looked like a man about to be hanged. "I guess we'll stay, Mr. Gatling. I know I will." He gave Gatling a feeble smile. "Maybe we're over the worst of it."

And if elephants had wings . . . Gatling thought, as he blew out the light and stretched out to sleep.

Chapter
EIGHT

By morning Wheeler had changed his mind about picking up the original route and following it southwest toward the sea. This was an unusual move, but nobody argued about it. No one was inclined to: It would keep them out of the jungle. Past the lake, the river twisted its way through flat country and on both sides of it were miles of tall, waving grass. Far ahead were more mountains.

They had buried their dead by the lake and moved on. Simms, the wounded surveyor, joined the dead before the sun came up. Mackenzie recited some words from the Bible. O'Sullivan had already photographed the lake and the islands in it, so there was nothing more to keep them there.

"We'll follow the river," Wheeler told his chief surveyor. "All you have to do is make adjustments in the survey done thus far. All we're doing here is groundwork."

"Yes, Mr. Wheeler," the surveyor said. Like everyone else, all he wanted to do was get to Panama City, on the Pacific coast. There a Navy ship was waiting to take them north to San Francisco. They would go back east by train.

Gatling didn't like the look of all that grassland. Not all of it was swamp, and where there was water it wouldn't be all that deep. Frobisher had the advantage of being able to travel

light. No tents, boxes of instruments and supplies, alcohol
stoves, cots, folding chairs. No queer secretaries, personal
cooks, newspaper scribblers. His men would eat cold food,
make cold camp, sleep on the ground, stop and go when and
where they pleased. If they went light on comfort, they'd go
heavy on rifles and ammunition. Gatling knew they'd never run
out of ammunition; it was the one thing he could be sure of.

Out beyond the grassland was a range of low hills. So low
that only the tops could be seen from the river, but high enough
to shoot from with long-range rifles. Right now there was a
heat haze that would make distance shooting difficult.
Frobisher's men could wait for the heat haze to disappear—it
usually lifted by early afternoon—or they could move in closer.
They'd have to come through all that grass and water, and there
were plenty of snakes in there, but that was what they were
being paid to do, and Frobisher would see that they did it if
that's what he decided. Frobisher would drive them like the
brutal officer he had been. You didn't get a job as big as this
one unless you had a record of getting things done.

If Wheeler's party was lucky, they'd get out of the grasslands
before Frobisher hit them—not that he couldn't do it anyplace
he picked. But this was bad country; it was made for hit-and-
run tactics. All they could do was get out of it as fast as possible.
Not so easy, though, not with all the junk they had to drag along.
He wondered if Wheeler could be reasoned with, could be
persuaded to ditch some of the dead weight that was slowing
them down. There was just too much of it. The trouble with
Wheeler was, he might agree to one thing when sober, then
change his mind when he got drunk. It would be easy to just
throw away the extra junk and let Wheeler take it any way he
liked. But Gatling knew he wouldn't do it because of Mackenzie,
who would be caught in the middle if Wheeler ordered him to
take some kind of action. The bastard might even order
Mackenzie to go back and look for the junk that had been thrown
away. One way or another, Mackenzie would be in a rotten fix.
He had nothing but contempt for Wheeler, but he was under
orders to do anything Wheeler ordered him to do. If he went

against orders, he could be charged with mutiny, and the punishment for that was a long stretch in a Navy prison.

Behind him he heard Wheeler calling a halt, then he heard him arguing with Irby, who kept urging him to move on until they found a safer place to rest. "Those Marines have to rest," Wheeler roared. "I won't have those men abused. You try carrying what they're carrying and we'll see how peppy you are. I say we rest."

"But it's not safe, Dock," Irby said. "Mackenzie says they could shoot at us from those hills back there. A perfect place to shoot from, Mackenzie says."

"What's that? What hills?" Wheeler didn't see much of anything when he had enough booze in him. "Why did Mackenzie talk to you and not to me? Aw, the hell with it! We won't rest. If it'll make you feel any better, we'll keep going till our balls drop off. Fair enough, Irb? You tell those poor, suffering Marines no rest because you and Mackenzie got together and decided not to."

Wheeler roared loud enough to be heard far beyond the column. Whenever he wanted to sit on his fat ass it was always for the sake of the poor, suffering Marines—not that the men weren't grateful for any rest they could get, but even the dumbest of them knew that sprawling around in the wrong places could get them killed. Gatling knew they were bewildered by Wheeler's carryings-on because, young or not-so-young, recent recruits or old sweats, they'd never seen anyone like Wheeler before. They looked to Mackenzie to make some sense out of it. He was tough but fair, and they respected him for that.

They moved on for another three miles, then Mackenzie dropped back from the lead and told Wheeler his men needed a 15-minute rest. That got Wheeler started again. "You didn't want to rest back there. Why do you want to rest now? Getting too much for you, is it?"

Gatling didn't turn to look; he could hear it all plain enough. The son of a bitch, he thought. The drunken, loudmouth son of a bitch!

Mackenzie was saying, "They can manage without a rest if

the civilians will spell them for a while."

"I can't agree to that," Wheeler roared. "Your men have
their pride, and I won't be the one to take it away from them.
How do you think they'd feel if they saw civilians doing a job
that is rightfully theirs? I'm surprised you don't realize that,
Mackenzie. We'll give them their hard-earned rest."

"Fifteen minutes," Mackenzie said.

"I'll decide how long," Wheeler said furiously, then flopped
down on the folding stool that Fritz, his cook and man of all
work, always had ready for him. Irby moved in close and began
to whisper. Gatling figured the secretary was trying to talk some
sense into him, something he hadn't seen before. Maybe Irby
realized, for the first time, the danger they were in, that *he* was
in. Irby was an arrogant man, deferring only to Wheeler, and
like all self-centered men he probably thought of death as
something that happened to other people. But now, from the
looks of it, he seemed to have reluctantly accepted the hard fact
that it could happen to him, and so he was urging caution.

Wheeler didn't roar, but he spoke loud enough to be heard
by everyone. "Don't piss your pants, Irb. We've got the finest
bunch of men, military and civilian, ever assembled in one
outfit. Let the bastards come. We took care of those fucking
indios, didn't we? Goddamned right we did."

But for all his bullshit, Wheeler gave the order to move before
the 15 minutes were up. Good for Irby, Gatling thought. They
could use all the help they could get, even from a drawling
queer. It didn't matter a damn that Wheeler listened to Irby
instead of Mackenzie. Gatling knew Mackenzie didn't care. He
was no ass-kisser, didn't have to prove anything; all he wanted
to do was to save as many of his men as he could. More of
them would die, no doubt about that, but if only a handful
survived, Mackenzie would look after them.

O'Sullivan caught up with Gatling, who was carrying the case
with the light gun in it. The automatic rifle was slung across
his back. He was right behind the Marines, carrying the mortar
and shells, the Maximite and fuses, and extra ammunition for
the light gun and rifle.

"The civilians are acting kind of funny," O'Sullivan said without taking the cigar out of his mouth. Now that he was back to smoking, he smoked all the time. "Have you noticed it?"

"Not particularly," Gatling answered. "Who wouldn't act kind of funny in this stinking country?"

They were making good time. Mackenzie was pushing the men, but they knew why, so it was all right. So far, so good, Gatling thought. In an hour or two they'd be clear of the grasslands, and the base of the mountains would provide some protection. Anything was better than open country.

"I heard that Engineer Jones came to see you last night. No, I wasn't sneaking about in the dark. I heard them talking. To them I'm just an idiot photographer."

Gatling had given his word to Jones and wasn't going to go back on it. He would tell Mackenzie, but that wasn't the same thing. O'Sullivan didn't have to know about it. Neither did anyone else. If it got back to Wheeler there would be hell to pay.

"Jones wanted to borrow a rifle," Gatling said. "He thinks I'm a walking arsenal. I told him no."

O'Sullivan gave Gatling a sidelong look. "Jones is chomping at the bit, is he? Wants to get into the thick of battle? By the look of him, that's a bit hard to believe. To me, he looks as nervous as a cat."

"So was Bill Hickok, nervous as a cat. He'd draw at a loud noise. That's why he killed so many men. Nervous."

O'Sullivan laughed softly. "You wouldn't be trying to change the subject, would you?"

"What were we talking about, Tim?"

"Engineer Jones, the latter-day warrior. You say he wanted the loan of a rifle. You sure he didn't want Daddy to kiss it and make it well? I mean his timid little soul."

"Jones is all right. So are the rest of them. They just joined the wrong expedition, is all. They did pretty good with those Indians."

Gatling couldn't think of any other nice things to say about the civilians. Some of them were a pain in the ass. The way they talked to the Marines, for one thing. That was the way they were brought up, but a man didn't have to go through life accepting everything he'd been taught as a child. A man could learn to think for himself.

"They fought because they had to," O'Sullivan said, smiling his mean smile. "It was fight or get killed. Worse than killed, I'd say, from the look of those colorfully painted bushmen."

"Best way to fight," Gatling said, "is when your own life depends on it. Fighting for other people's lives takes a different kind of courage."

"Like yours?"

"Hell, no, Tim. I get well paid for doing what I do. Nice day, isn't it?"

It wasn't any kind of nice. No day in Darien was nice. Winter or summer, spring or fall, every day was lousy.

O'Sullivan said, "It can't have escaped your notice that the great man and his amanuensis have been having their tense moments."

The Irishman had little formal education, but he read a lot and liked to pepper his conversation with unfamiliar words and phrases. When this show of learning was added to his Irish tough talk, it startled people who didn't know him. Maybe that was what he intended.

"Irby's been trying to calm him down," Gatling said. "More power to him, is what I say. Wheeler doesn't like it, being what he is, but I think maybe he's starting to listen."

O'Sullivan removed a shred of tobacco from his teeth. "Rotten cheap cigars. If I'd only known . . . You know it's not going to last. He's scared now because he knows he can get smashed in the mouth with a bullet at any moment. But mark my words, Herr Gatling, as soon as he feels himself out of danger he'll go back to dancing around the maypole."

Gatling had to smile. "What's wrong with that, Timothy?" He knew O'Sullivan hated to be called Timothy. "If I thought we were out of danger I'd probably join him."

"The ladies wouldn't like it," O'Sullivan said. "And neither would the divine Sarah."

Sergeant O'Hara was killed just as it was getting dark. If it had been 30 minutes later they wouldn't have been able to see him or anyone else. He gasped and dropped and died without making another sound, shot through the neck. The boom of the big-caliber long-range rifle sounded an instant later.

"Down!" Mackenzie shouted. "Everybody down. Down flat."

Flat in the mud, Gatling raised up a little. There was no more shooting after the first shot. At first he thought it might be the signal for an attack from closer in. The single shot had fired from high ground a long way off. He could tell by the sound. He had the light gun out of the case and ready to fire. There wasn't a sound except for the hot wind rattling the tall reeds in the swamp. The sky was darkening as the sun started to slide toward the far side of the mountains. Wheeler and Irby were down in the mud with the rest of them. It had been so quiet a few moments before. The great man looked confused. It was quiet now. O'Sullivan started to say something. Gatling told him to shut up. Mackenzie was crawling toward them.

"You think they'll try anything more?" Mackenzie said, wiping off the gun barrel on the sleeve of his jacket.

"Not too likely," Gatling said. "I figure they just got here from Colon. Probably took the train, then crossed the river ahead of us. I'm just guessing."

"Sounds right enough. If they got here earlier we'd have heard from them. Best we can do is wait here till it gets dark. Bastards can't shoot if they can't see. Not unless they get closer."

The sun was a red glare behind the mountain peaks. "I figure Frobisher isn't organized yet. He's got plenty of time to do that. We're not going to run away," Gatling said.

"Even if we could," Mackenzie added. "Goddamn it, our numbers are dwindling fast. O'Hara was a real old soldier, one of the best."

The light faded abruptly, and they got up out of the mud and moved on. Gatling heard Wheeler cursing and complaining. He had thrown himself down so hard he was covered with mud from head to foot. "Jesus Christ, Irb, I feel like I've been rolling around in a hog wallow." Gatling couldn't hear Irb's reply, but figured it was soft and soothing. Just the same, there would be no hot food for the great man tonight; he would have to sleep on the ground with the rest of them. No lights, no tents. Tents made shapes to shoot at, even in the dark. This was one time when Wheeler wasn't going to get his own way. Mackenzie told Gatling he was going to lay down certain rules, and if Wheeler broke them, then he was going to put him under restraint.

"If he shows a light or insists on erecting a tent, that'll be it." Mackenzie's eyes were worried, but his jaw was set. "Oh, I don't mind taking his usual drunken bullshit, but this is different. I can't let the dirty sot risk the lives of these people. I'd be no man and no officer if I let that happen. I pray he'll listen to his fancy man, or whatever you call him. If he can't control him, I will. It'll be the end of me in the Corps, but perhaps they won't send me to prison, just kick me out on my backside. I can always work at something."

Gatling couldn't think of much to say. What he did say was, "If there's a court-martial and I'm still alive, I'll be there. So will O'Sullivan, maybe a few other people." Gatling wanted Mackenzie to know that he could count on a few friends. But even as he said it he had made up his mind to kill Wheeler long before he could run squealing to Mackenzie's commanding officer. Some dark night . . .

The shooting started again before they cleared the swamp, and this time there were no aimed shots, just a lot of lead coming at them from behind. Gatling figured Frobisher's men had come down from the hills into the swamp, plowed through it in the dark, then climbed up out of it to harass them from the rear. Gatling pulled off his canvas coat, threw it on the muddy ground, and put the light gun on top of it. He told Mackenzie he'd cover them until they were out of the swamp and starting up the mountain slope. Up there were scattered rocks and fissures in the rock face that would provide cover.

"Do it, Mac," Gatling said before he lay down in the mud behind the gun. "They're far back, but they'll catch up fast."

"Don't stay too long," Mackenzie said, and disappeared into the dark. Bullets sang over Gatling's head as he waited for them to get closer. They were laying down heavy fire, and up ahead he heard somebody cry out. The moon hadn't showed yet, but there was some light, and a few minutes later he could make out fast-moving shapes coming toward him in the thickening dark. They fired as they ran, not stopping to squeeze off careful shots, because right now they were firing to create panic.

Like hell! Gatling opened fire and the men out in front went down in a tangle of arms and legs, screaming in pain and confusion. The attackers behind them tried to spread out, but he followed them with long and short bursts from the light gun. The light gun rattled and stopped and rattled again, and every time it did men went down, and if a few staggered back to their feet, the light gun hit them again. Suddenly the rest of them were all down flat in the mud and firing back at him, jacking bullets as fast as they could work the loading levers. The heaviest fire was coming from a stretch of tall reeds just below firm ground. The sons of bitches had all jumped in there together. He swung the gun and concentrated his fire on the place where they were bunched up. Gatling was firing blind—there was no longer anything solid to shoot at—but he knew the relentless force of the light gun would drive them back out into the swamp. The firing slacked off and stopped. There was yelling out there in the dark, then somebody shouted something and there were no sounds after that. The shouter would be Frobisher. Gatling picked up the light gun and ran. No bullets came after him.

Running through the mud, he nearly stumbled over a body that lay facedown and silent. No way to tell whose body it was. No time to check, too dark to be sure. He stepped over the body and kept running. When he heard them up ahead he slowed down to a walk. He'd have his balls in the ringer if he dropped the light gun in the mud. And it would be a bitch to get shot by mistake. He shouted his name and Mackenzie answered.

'Ahoy there, Gatling!" Mackenzie shouted back. "We hear you, Gatling! Permission to come aboard!"

Gatling caught up. He knew Mackenzie had been hanging

back, waiting to see if the light gun was enough to stop them.

"Who got killed back there?" Gatling asked him.

"Private Finnegan," Mackenzie said. "Just a kid. Stray bullet struck him in the back of the head. "Christ! I'm wondering if I'll get anybody back."

They squelched along in the mud. Gatling said, "Anybody else get hit?"

"Nobody. A few of the boxes got hit. No need to go into mourning. None of *your* boxes got hit. I checked on it myself. You think we have a chance?"

"I don't know, Mac. Let's get up there and see. I figure we can hold them off for a bit. I have a few surprises for Frobisher, but I won't spring them on him unless I have to. Depends how it goes."

They climbed the slope until they came to the bottom of a rock face that rose up for hundreds of feet. It sloped out near the top, so they couldn't be gotten at from above, even if Frobisher's men could climb that high. As long as they stayed under the overhang, no rocks could be rolled down on them and they were safe from gunfire.

A sort of natural stone wall ran along the base of the cliff, and most of it was protected by the overhang. It had a clear view of the slope, a good place to shoot from, and they could have holed up there for weeks if they had enough water. That was the principal problem: They didn't have enough water. They had started out with what seemed like enough at the time, but it hadn't turned out that way, and the water supply had already been running short by the time they reached the lake. Water from the lake could have been boiled and bottled if Wheeler hadn't ordered them to move on, saying they would do it later. That hadn't been done, and now they were in a place where there was no water at all.

For once, Wheeler was too rattled to tear into Mackenzie, who had become the scapegoat because he was the ranking officer. There was enough water to last them for about a week if they used it sparingly; after that they'd be in trouble. Food was a lesser problem, so nobody was too concerned; there was enough for now.

There was a small cave, its entrance hidden by dry brush, and Wheeler took possession as soon as he heard about it. He sent Irby and Fritz in to clear out the snakes, if there were any, while he sat on a rock drinking from his canteen. Before he moved in, with Fritz carrying his belongings, Mackenzie told him they wouldn't be showing lights of any kind. Wheeler began to bluster, but Mackenzie talked right over him, respectful but firm. Before Wheeler could start in on him, Mackenzie played his top card.

"Mr. Wheeler, those men have long-range rifles with telescopic sights. We show the faintest light and they'll sight in on it. A man standing in front of a light will be a dead duck. I daresay you'll be safe enough from direct fire, but think of the ricochets, sir."

Wheeler knew he was stumped, but he couldn't let it go. "What makes you think I'm going to show a light, for God's sake. If someone told you that, point him out, mister, and he'll get a tongue-lashing he'll never forget. Or is all this nonsense your idea? Answer up, man."

"It's standard procedure," Mackenzie said calmly, adding "sir" so Wheeler couldn't get at him for that. "Good night, Mr. Wheeler."

All he got was an ill-mannered grunt. Wheeler went into his cave, followed by Irby and the cook.

They ate their cold food and settled down for the night. Mackenzie posted all his men in two five-hour shifts; it wouldn't be light for ten hours. Gatling got a canvas coat from supplies and stretched out beside the light gun, which he covered with a rubber groundsheet.

Up where they were it was cooler than on the flat, and they might have slept if the shooting hadn't started up again about 30 minutes after they rolled up in their blankets. Mackenzie told his men not to return fire unless Frobisher's night-crawlers started up the slope. Gatling didn't think they would, and neither did Mackenzie.

"Frobisher is smarter than that," Gatling said. "What he'll try to do—will do—is wear us down."

Mackenzie nodded. He didn't have to be told.

The firing from below went on hour after hour, and it was no hail of lead but slow, steady shooting by several big-caliber rifles, maybe Remington Rolling Blocks or Big Fifty Sharps. Rifles like those didn't crack, they boomed like small cannons. God help you if you got hit with a chunk of lead from one of those monsters. Buffalo hunters liked them because they could knock down a bull buffalo with one shot. If a man got hit in the arm, then he had the arm torn from his body. They could blow a man's spine out through his back.

Mackenzie told everybody to stay flat and as close to the rock barrier as they could get. A young mapmaker named du Pre got cut in the face by rock splinters, but no one else was injured by ricochets. So far, nobody was in any great danger from bullets. The real damage, and it was considerable, was to their nerves as lead smacked against rock without any letup. Now and then there would be a lull in the shooting, but it always picked up again.

They had to get out of there, but they couldn't get out tonight. Gatling went to sleep beside the light gun while the unseen enemy continued to fire at them. As long as he wasn't in any immediate danger, he could sleep through most anything.

He woke up to see Sarah Morrison crawling toward him, and she crawled in between him and the rock barrier without a word. He had to smile: She was using him as a shield.

Bullets were still hitting rocks; nothing had changed since he'd drifted off to sleep. His back was turned to her, and he kept it that way. He felt her shaking.

"Comfortable enough?" he asked her.

He felt the vigorous nodding of her head. "Yes," she said in a faint voice.

"Then try to get some sleep," he ordered. "No talk about this or that or anything. I've got a lot of thinking to do."

Chapter
NINE

Gatling hadn't found any answers by the time Sarah Morrison woke up and complained that she hadn't been able to sleep a wink all night. "Christ on the Cross, Gatling, I'm going to go crazy if we don't get out of here soon. There's nothing worse than not getting any sleep."

The sun was coming up, sending streaks of light across the sky. An occasional bullet still hit the rock face above them, bringing down little showers of splintered stone. The Marines who had stood the first watch were asleep. Some of the civilians had spent the night sitting up, their heads drooping with fatigue, their eyes staring with fright.

"You were just pretending to sleep to make me feel better," Gatling said. "I appreciate that."

She ignored that. "Can't you think of anything that'll get us out of here? You're the great troubleshooter from out West. Can't you come up with some sort of plan?"

Another bullet hit the rock, and some of the civilians stared at the rock fragments as they fell. Frobisher was easing up a bit, Gatling thought. That was how you did it. You eased up, gave your enemy a short period of calm, and then you hit him worse than before.

Gatling said, "My only plan right now is to get something

to eat. Like a can of beans, with maybe peaches in syrup to follow. Sound good to you?''

No sounds came from Wheeler's cave. No doubt the great man had drunk himself into a stupor and still lay sleeping on his cot. Wheeler and Irby were in there, but not Fritz; the cook and man of all work had slept outside under a blanket, with the mosquitoes and the bullets.

"Sounds rotten," Sarah Morrison said. "All I want is a drink of water. When will the goddamned coffee be ready?''

"When it's ready. Don't look for any fancy cooking up here. You'll be lucky if you get coffee. In the meantime, here's my canteen.''

She drank from it, then gave it back to him. "Jumping Jesus, mister, I never thought water could taste so bad.''

Gatling drank some water, just enough to quench his thirst, and then he stoppered the canteen and put the strap over his shoulder. You could go a long time without food; without water you were dead in days.

She was frowning at him when he looked at her. "Any kind of water will taste like chilled champagne if you're up here long enough. What's the sour face all about? I didn't gag and bind you and drag you here.''

"Nobody said you did. But how's about getting me out of here?''

"Just you? Nobody else?''

"You know what I mean, so put a cork in the joke bottle. Listen to me, you yokel. You were paid to protect us and you haven't done a very good job of it. My father is an investor, so that makes me an investor. I demand protection, you son of a bitch.''

Suddenly he realized that she was close to hysterics, and no wonder she'd been so subdued the night before. Women often get very quiet before they came apart at the seams. She was a bitch's bitch, but she was right about one thing: He owed her protection.

"You swore you'd get me safe home and look where I am.'' She started to cry. Oh, Christ! Gatling thought. This is just what

I need. She had her bag with her, and he opened it and took out her liquor flask. She looked at him, tears running down her face, while he unscrewed the cap and filled it with brandy. Her hands were shaking so hard, he had to hold the cap to her mouth while she drank. He filled it again and she drank it.

"That's not the answer," she said, but changed her mind as the brandy started to take effect. "Thanks, Gatling. You're still a heartless bastard, but you can't help that, can you?"

No shots had been fired for five minutes. Frobisher was letting them get comfortable before he pulled the rug out from under. Gatling thought of a few things he'd like to do to William Frobisher.

"Have tried to change my savage nature," he told Sarah Morrison. "But it's no good. Ought to go back and live with my own kind. Wolverines and grizzly bears."

She fixed the next drink by herself. "You're such an idiot," she said, knocking back the brandy like a veteran. The brandy calmed her and cheered her, but didn't make her drunk. Fear was hard to overcome. He was glad to see her in control of herself. No more tears. She even smiled. Lord protect me from wailing women, he thought.

Another smile, "I know you'll think of something," she said.

Gatling said he'd do his best.

"That's good enough for me." She seemed to mean it. "I think I'd like to sleep now. I did sleep, but it was worse than no sleep. Such dreams."

Wheeler called a conference in his cave, which made Mackenzie smile in spite of the bad fix they were in. There wasn't room for everybody, so only the "senior men," as Wheeler called them, were allowed to attend. These were Tabor, Mackenzie, Gatling, and Garth. Sarah Morrison and Bateman Olds weren't there, and neither was Dr. LaPlante, who regarded it as none of his business, and said so.

The sun was high in the sky, and it was all right to have fires. Fritz had brewed coffee on an alcohol stove, and Wheeler and Irby were drinking it. A hurricane lantern stood on a packing case, giving off harsh yellow light.

Outside, the shooting had started up again; Wheeler winced every time a bullet hit the rock. "Gentlemen," he began. "We are in a precarious position. The question is, how are we to get out of it? Mr. Gatling, we'll start with you. Do you have any ideas?"

Gatling said, "I have one idea, but it depends on your cooperation." Wheeler gave a noncommittal grunt. Gatling took a stick of Maximite from his pocket and held it up. "This is the most powerful explosive ever developed. The Maxim Company makes it, and if you haven't heard of it, it's because it's so new it isn't on the market yet."

Wheeler didn't want to admit there was something he didn't know, so he said, "Of course I've heard of it. But go on."

Gatling said, "It's fifty percent more powerful than dynamite. That's fact, but you'll have to take my word for it."

"What do you propose to do with it, Mr. Gatling? Blow the mountain down on top of Frobisher and his thugs?"

Only Tabor smiled.

"More or less, that's what I intend to do," Gatling went on. Having to talk so much didn't set well with him, but he had to make the great man, the booze-soaked idiot, understand. "Frobisher will attack this position sooner or later. He doesn't know how much water and food we have, and he won't wait down there forever. That's my opinion, but I could be wrong."

"What if you are?" Wheeler asked. "Whatever it is you're talking about."

Gatling wouldn't let himself be riled. "He could wait us out, just sit there till our water and food are gone. If he waits long enough, all he'll have to do is climb up here and shoot those of us that aren't dead."

Wheeler didn't like to hear that kind of talk. He took a short drink from his flask.

"I don't think he'll wait," Gatling said. "Our job, if you agree to it, is to convince him that he doesn't have to waste his time out there in the hot sun with the mosquitoes eating at him."

Wheeler took another short pull at his flask; the son of a bitch was making some effort not to get drunk, but Gatling wasn't sure his good intentions would last out the day.

"What the hell are you talking about?" Wheeler looked ready to bust a gut. "You want him to attack us, is that what I understood you to say?"

"That's right. We have to make him think we're so weak and down in the mouth that he'll come charging up that slope with all his troops. If we can convince him to do that, we can put him out of business for good."

Gatling still had the stick of Maximite in his hand, and he held it up. "This will do it."

Wheeler gave an unpleasant laugh. "One stick will do all that?"

"I have a whole box of it," Gatling said.

"Then show us what it can do," Wheeler said. "If you have a whole box, you can spare one stick. Go on out and throw it down the mountain. Let the bastards see what we have up here."

Gatling wondered if Wheeler's brain had gone soft with alcohol. That had to be it; he couldn't be that stupid.

"The whole point here is surprise," Gatling said. "If Frobisher knows what we have, he won't come near the place till we're half dead from thirst and hunger."

Irby leaned forward to whisper in Wheeler's ear. The next question was Irby's question. Wheeler said, "How is this thing to be accomplished? How are we to convince Frobisher that we're so low in spirits we'll agree to anything? Send him down a note saying we aren't feeling well?"

Gatling knew the last part was Wheeler's. "Not just low in spirits. That's not enough. We have to convince him that we have no water left. That's the main thing—the water. If we don't get water we die. That's how he has to see it."

Wheeler's folding stool creaked under his bulk. "You still haven't answered the question. Before we can convince him of anything, we first have to talk to the man."

"I'll do it," Gatling said.

"And what will you tell him?"

"At first I won't tell him anything. What I'll be doing down there is pretending to look for a deal. Something like if he lets us go, we'll abandon the expedition, dump instruments, maps, everything, and head for the coast. My approach will be the hell with the fucking expedition, just let us go."

"And he'll just naturally believe you?"

"Why not? I'll bitch like hell. Tell him I was a fool to join the expedition in the first place. It's all fucked up, I'll tell him. I'll have to paint a black picture of you, Mr. Wheeler. You have to be the villain. You have to be most of the reason why the people who work for you want to get away from here anyway they can."

Wheeler stared at Gatling, trying to decide whether he was being made a fool of. Finding it hard to decide, he took a short drink.

"All right," he said. "What if he agrees? And what do *we* do? Go down there and let ourselves be killed?"

"We don't do a thing. If he lets me go, I'll come back up here. I'm just a messenger boy. You're the one who has to decide."

"And what do I decide?" Wheeler put a sneer in his voice.

"You don't decide," Gatling said. "You want to get out of here, but can't make up your mind if you can trust Frobisher. You weasel. You blow hot and cold. But you can't make up your mind."

A mosquito buzzed around Wheeler's sweaty face and he slapped at it. Then he pouted like a huge baby. "Frobisher will never believe that if he knows anything about me."

Gatling pushed ahead. "You've changed, and for the worse. Something or other has made you fearful and indecisive. When Frobisher gets tired of waiting for an answer, he'll attack. He'll attack because he'll think he won't meet much opposition. That's when I'll hit him with the Maximite. It may not kill all his gunmen. It'll kill enough."

Irby whispered something else in Wheeler's ear. The great man sat up straight on his stool. "What about that machine gun of yours. You used it on Frobisher's men just last night. He'll know you and the gun are up here. Will he want to attack a machine gun?''

Wheeler had a point, Gatling had to admit. Or Irby did. "Not likely," Gatling said. "I'll have to think of something. The man with the machine gun was killed by a ricochet and nobody else knows how to operate the weapon. It has to sound right."

"Damn right it does," Mackenzie said, interrupting. "You're a dead man if it doesn't. But it's still a good plan."

"I was about to say it's a plan with possibilities." Wheeler scowled at Mackenzie. "But I have to think about it. I can see one thing wrong with it."

Gatling asked him what it was. There were plenty of things wrong with the plan, but he wanted to hear what Wheeler had to say.

"What if Frobisher knows you? I mean, knows what you look like?"

"I doubt if he knows more than my name. Frobisher himself is just a name to me, with a few bare facts on the side. I'm probably the same to him. I think it's worth the risk."

"You'll be the one taking it," Wheeler said. "You don't want to do this right away?"

"Too soon. The end of the week would be about right. By then we won't have to pretend our water is running short."

"Is that all of it?" It was obvious that Wheeler wanted them gone from his cave. Danger or no danger, he could settle down to a day of drinking. Let the bullets fly. He would keep the bullets at bay with brandy.

"There is something else," Gatling said, disregarding the great man's scowl. "It concerns all the things the Marines have to carry. There's just too much of it, it slows us down, it breaks their backs. I'd like to get rid of three quarters of it."

Wheeler lurched up off his stool, threatening to collapse it by his sudden movement. He shook his meaty fist in Gatling's face. "Have you gone crazy? Do you know what you're saying? This expedition was planned right down to the last detail. Nothing was brought along that we didn't need and still need. And now you want to throw about three quarters of our valuable supplies, our camping equipment, our . . .''

Irby did some more whispering. Wheeler nodded. "How can you ask such a thing, Gatling. I'm surprised at you. You certainly don't have to carry anything."

Gatling said, "It's no good killing Frobisher if we don't lighten our load. We can blow big holes in his outfit, but that's not to say every man jack will be killed. Frobisher could be lucky and survive. If he does he'll be coming after us. Our main objective is to break out of here without getting killed. I'm pretty sure that can be done. But what good is breaking out if we can't move faster? The way we creep along, we could have a two-day start and he'd still catch up to us. I can't see any way out of it. We have to abandon most of what we brought."

Wheeler was so enraged that he got up and walked around the cave. Garth and others got out of his way. Suddenly he stopped and pointed at Gatling, like a stage character about to wither another character in his boots.

"What you're asking me to do is to abandon an expedition that has taken a year to finance and organize. Of all the colossal nerve, yours is by far the winner. Do you know what you're asking me to do? I hardly think so. Oh, why am I wasting my time with a man like you?"

Wheeler dropped his loud voice to a loud whisper. He got up real close so Gatling couldn't mistake what he was saying. "The answer is no. Did you hear me? No. The answer is no."

"Then forget about the plan. One thing depends on the other. I can break you out of here, probably I can, but it won't mean anything. You're as good as dead. If we can't move fast, we might as well forget about it. Even if we get away from Frobisher, we'll be coming into rebel country pretty soon. Give it some thought. You don't have that much time left."

Gatling went out before Wheeler became more indignant, more enraged. The Marines had coffee going behind the rock barrier; since the death of Private Maddocks, who had been their cook, they managed any way they could. One of the men who died of yellow fever had cooked for the civilians. They were in the same boat, but not handling it half as well.

Gatling usually ate with the Marines. Their manners were

down-to-earth, if not downright dirty, and they had a better sense of humor. None of them hoped to become Commandant of the Corps, or an officer of even the lowest rank, and so free of ambition, they enjoyed life in their own way. They had been paid 15 dollars a month until a thrifty Congress, ever aware of the need to balance the budget, reduced their pay to 13.

Gatling drank truly bad coffee until Wheeler's conference broke up and Mackenzie came out with a scornful look on his face. Mackenzie ducked his head as he came along the inside of the rock barrier. Ducking like that was something they were all learning to do. It was duck your head or maybe get it blown off.

Mackenzie hunkered down by the tiny fire and poured himself a cup of coffee. He made an even worse face than the one he'd left the conference with. "My Lord! This stuff tastes as bad as the water. No, it's worse. These Marines have a way of ruining everything they touch. They could burn cole slaw."

Mackenzie paused to sip his coffee. "I'm pretty sure Wheeler will come around to your way of thinking. He knows you're right. He just doesn't want to admit it. He wants to go back to New York covered with glory. The way things are going, he'll be lucky to get there at all. You know, I feel sorry for him in a way. It must be miserable to see something like this go down the shithole. All I can say is—and I'm not being mealymouthed—he did it to himself. Some things he obviously couldn't control, but he should've come with his head screwed on. If the booze had an iron grip on him, he should have stayed home."

Gatling didn't want to hear any more about Wheeler's life as a drunk. It seemed like too many people spent too much time talking about goddamned Murdock Wheeler. Let the son of a bitch go to a rest home, one of those country places for loonies and drunks, and take the cure.

"But he didn't stay home," Gatling said. "He's here and we have to deal with him. How about if I take over? That'll leave you in the clear. You can bet the civilians won't object."

Mackenzie topped up his cup with bad coffee. "It wouldn't

work, Gatling. I'd still be court-martialed. I'm thinking maybe I should seize power, so to speak, then lose myself when we get to the coast. There's lots of places I can go. South America. I've always wanted to see South America.''

"Wait till you retire. You're not cut out for the other.''

Mackenzie sighed. "I suppose not. But what are we going to do. We could kill the bastard.''

"Are you serious?''

"You think I'm not? You're forgetting I went right through the Civil War when I was just a kid, and I can tell you many's the mean or incompetent officer got shot by accident on purpose. Same situation here. Not one bit of difference.''

Sarah Morrison was still asleep by the light gun. Her face was dirty and her clothes were stained, but she looked fine. Too bad she's so crazy, Gatling thought.

"We'll wait out the rest of the week,'' Gatling said. "Maybe Irby can talk some sense into him by then. Maybe he'll change his mind when he wakes up one morning and there's no water.''

"He'll just go on drinking booze.''

"No, he won't. We're going to get rid of it.''

Mackenzie laughed. "Lord, but you *are* a cruel man. How're we going to do it?''

"I don't know, Mac. Put your thinking cap on and help me out. There's no point talking to Wheeler when he's drunk. You heard him in there today.''

"Did I ever. You're right, you know. But he'll be like a wild man when he finds his booze gone. I don't look forward to it. Even so, it has to be done. Maggie Bacon will be proud of us.''

Maggie Bacon was a grim-faced lady from Kansas who went around the country wrecking saloons with a hatchet she kept in a flowered carpetbag.

"We have to get Irby and Tabor out of the way,'' Gatling said.

"We'll think of something,'' Mackenzie said. "What I like about this is, he won't be able to prove a thing. He can't whistle up the Chief of Detectives. I'm beginning to enjoy this already.''

Two lead slugs smacked the wall, but Mackenzie didn't seem to notice.

"Keep your goddamned head down," Gatling said.

"Be a pity to lose it when things are starting to go right for a change."

They haven't gone right yet, Gatling thought. It was all right to joke with Mackenzie, but Frobisher and his killers were still out there.

"Here's to crime," Mackenzie said, raising his coffee mug.

"Cheers!" Gatling said.

Chapter
TEN

"Who stole my liquor?" Wheeler roared, pacing up and down his cave, red-faced, trembling, absolutely furious. "I want to know who sneaked in here and stole my liquor." The great man tried to get a grip on himself, and failed. He needed a drink, and would have killed to get it. He went back and forth between bullying and begging—not that he really begged, but there was a whine in his voice that told them how bad off he was.

All his "senior men" were there: Tabor, Mackenzie, Gatling, Garth. Dr. LaPlante was there too, and for two reasons: The doctor was worried about Wheeler, and even he had come under suspicion.

It was morning, a very bad morning for Wheeler. It was a bad morning for everybody. A hurricane lantern stood on a packing case, and beside it a mug of coffee was getting cold. Now and then Wheeler looked at the coffee mug; there should have been a big dollop of brandy in his morning coffee, but there wasn't. All the liquor had disappeared.

Wheeler picked up the coffee mug, sipped at it, then hurled it against the wall of the cave. The coffee ran down the wall and made a puddle on the floor. Except for Wheeler, nobody moved. Irby sat on the folding stool, his face blank, his eyes hooded.

Wheeler stopped pacing and tried the good-fellow approach. He tried for a smile, but his face fell apart, and he shook like a man with fever.

"Look," he said in a voice that shook like the rest of him. "A joke is a joke, but now it's time to be serious. We aren't little kids, are we, and I find it disturbing to have to treat you as such. It could be said that I drink a little too much at times, and there are some of you who disapprove of that." He paused to scowl at the doctor. "But I never have been what you might call *drunk*. Nor have I ever been irresponsible, careless, or incompetent. A man in my position is under a terrible strain. There is just too much responsibility for one man. So I drink a little. It's my way of relaxing after a strenuous day. Those men who died . . . Sometime soon I must sit down and write letters to their families. Think of that."

The doctor said, "Mr. Wheeler, you must try to calm down. Your blood pressure—"

"The hell with blood pressure. What do I care about blood pressure. And I'll thank you to keep your godblasted medicine to yourself. I don't want it."

Earlier, after the theft of the liquor was discovered, Dr. LaPlante had tried to get the great man to take a sedative, and had come close to being assaulted. Now he stood with the others, like a criminal before the bar of justice.

Gatling thought Wheeler looked like a starving man standing outside a fancy restaurant. All that mouth-watering food in there, and no way to get at it. So near and yet so far.

It had been a pretty slick job, he decided. They'd gotten the liquor out by putting snakes in. He caught the snakes himself, when they came out of the rocks to bask in the sun. Two big rattlers, thick-bodied and dangerous. In the dim light of dawn, he released the two snakes, and they crawled under the blanket that was hung over the mouth of the cave. He moved away and waited with Mackenzie.

A few minutes later Wheeler came howling out of the cave, followed by Irby. The great man was half drunk and scared out of his wits. Like many people, he was afraid of snakes; his red face was blotched with white and he ran as far as he could get. Bullets were still hitting the rock, and he might have been killed if a burly Marine hadn't jumped on his back and brought him crashing down.

In the uproar that followed, the liquor disappeared, and so did Wheeler's flask.

Now, two hours later, he was still going at it. He tried everything—threats, jokes, cajolery—but nothing worked. He sent Irby to get a drink from Sarah Morrison, but the secretary came back empty-handed.

"No more left," Irby said. "Or so she says. She could be lying."

Gatling knew she wasn't. He had spilled out her liquor while she clawed at him like a tigress. It took a while to settle her down, but after he explained how it was, she agreed that he had done the right thing. She wanted to live more than she wanted to drink.

Wheeler was off on another tangent. "Gentlemen," he declared, sweating like a bull. "I am prepared to strike a bargain with the rascal who has hidden my two cases of brandy. Bring it back, leave it outside, and no more will be said. I think that's a sensible solution to our problem, don't you? There need be no embarrassment on anybody's part. Mr. Irby and I will remain so as not to catch the culprit in the act. That's all, gentlemen."

Gatling was aware that Irby had been watching him while the great man ranted and raved. Now and then he darted a quick look at Mackenzie. The drawling queer had put it together, Gatling decided. The son of a bitch *knew*. So far he hadn't said anything, or Wheeler would have charged at them like a mad bull. Maybe he'd continue to keep his mouth shut; getting the great man off the bottle would benefit Irby just as much as the rest of them.

O'Sullivan said, "Wheeler is suffering from what Bowery folk call The Frights. But since he's a gentleman, let's say he has a bad case of *delirium tremens*. In short, he is seeing pink elephants. And snakes. Don't forget the snakes. You should have let me in on it. I would have been glad to help."

O'Sullivan was fishing. Gatling said, "I don't know what you're talking about. You know, Mac?"

"Haven't a clue." Mackenzie turned to O'Sullivan. "You haven't been drinking Mr. Wheeler's stolen brandy, have you? You talk as if you have."

They were hunkered down, drinking Marine coffee. There wouldn't be much more coffee after this: Their water was running low, and coffee-making wasn't the best way to conserve what was left.

Dr. LaPlante had been in and out of the cave several times during the day. Wheeler had been yelling, but now he was quiet; the doctor had given him an injection while Fritz and Irby held him down.

It was four days after Gatling told Wheeler about his plan for getting rid of Frobisher. "We'll wait two more days," he said. "We can't drag it out longer than that. We need water. If Wheeler hasn't recovered by then, I'll go ahead with it. But I'd just as soon have Wheeler on our side."

"I hope he dies, " O'Sullivan said. "The big man's passing would solve a lot of problems."

Mackenzie frowned. Sometimes the Irishman got on his nerves. "Rarely do men die of the d.t.'s. They may feel like they're dying, but they have to be far gone before they do. What Wheeler is dying for is a drink."

"I could go in your place," O'Sullivan said to Gatling. "You look a bit too resolute to go whining to Frobisher with surrender proposals. Let me go instead. I can whine and complain with the best of them. One look at me and Frobisher will know this outfit is falling apart."

Gatling smiled. "Can't let you do it, Tim. I have to see what they have down there."

"What could they have? An ice cream stall? Cold beer?" The Irishman had turned sarcastic.

"You left out Irish stew," Mackenzie said.

Gatling said, "I appreciate the offer, Tim, but I have to get some idea of how many men Frobisher has. I may not get to see anything. But I have to try.''

"Will you listen to the man,'' O'Sullivan said. Wheeler was awake and yelling. "The doc'll have to use a horse syringe if he keeps this up.''

Mackenzie said to Gatling, "Have you considered the possibility that Frobisher may shoot you down before you even get close?''

"I figure he'll want to talk,'' Gatling said. "What can he lose by talking?''

"Nothing. But you could lose your life if he isn't in a talking mood. Let me finish. Frobisher knows he holds all the cards, so he may not want to dicker, even pretend to dicker, for any deal he makes will be worthless.''

"I know that, for Christ's sake. I still say he'll want to talk.''

"Will you listen to me.'' Mackenzie was getting mad. "He may not want to talk because he may think we're not worth it. He may be a man who likes to see people suffer. Pretty soon that's what we'll be doing up here.''

Gatling said, "You just defeated your own argument, Mac. What's the difference of dying from a bullet down there or from thirst up here?''

O'Sullivan stuck a cigar in his mouth. "We could all commit suicide, like the Jews at Masada. We're the Jews, see. Frobisher is the Roman general Silva. We don't have poison, like the Jews, but we're up high enough to jump. . . .''

Mackenzie scowled his annoyance. "I have a great idea. You go first. You jump off right now. If the fall kills you, then we'll try it.''

Gatling said, "I think the sun is getting to both of you.''

"This photographer is getting to me,'' Mackenzie said. "It's all set then? You won't change your mind? I see the need of it, but I don't have to like it.''

"Neither do I,'' Gatling said.

Gatling got to the bottom of the slope and stood waiting. It had taken some time to climb down from the high ground. On that first night they had climbed up the side of the mountain, but he didn't want to go back that way; it would use up the best part of an hour. So he came down straight, and in places he had to hang and drop and skitter on his backside in the crumbling shale. Once, when the shale began to slide, he thought he'd be swept down and buried under thousands of tons of shale and sand and rock.

He waited in the fierce sun, and in his hand he carried a surveyor's rod with a white handkerchief tied to it. His flag of truce. The handkerchief was very white; it was one of the few clean ones Sarah Morrison had left.

Earlier he had waved his white flag, sticking it up over the top of the rock barrier. The sharpshooters might be in a bad mood. They might blow his head off and tell Frobisher about it later. At first he didn't think they'd seen the flag, but then the random shooting stopped and, in a few minutes, a white flag was waved from the edge of the swamp that came in close at the bottom of the mountain.

Gatling handed his binoculars to Mackenzie and started down, thinking they could kill him any time now. With telescopic sights, how could they miss? He felt like a fly on the side of the mountain, but in the telescopic sight fitted to a powerful rifle he would be man-sized. They could follow him with their sights, moving the sights as he came down the side of the mountain. These shooters would be the best money could buy; big business didn't weasel when a big job had to be done.

Nobody had waved at him since he got down from the mountain. Then a white flag waved and he started forward, not knowing he was doing the right thing, but figuring they wanted him to come in. They sure were careful, though not a single shot had been fired at them from up on the mountain.

When he got close to the tangle of brush and vine hung trees an American voice said, "Come ahead. Keep moving. That's it." Gatling walked in under the trees, and suddenly there was a man and a rifle behind him.

There was a small clearing on dry ground with men standing around with rifles in their hands. Other men were talking not far off. It sounded like a lot of men. Gatling knew there could be more. Frobisher's bosses wouldn't stint on the money, so he could hire all the men he wanted.

Frobisher himself came ducking his head, brushing creepers away from his face. Gatling knew he couldn't be anyone else; authority was stamped all over him. He had a long, thin face and a mean mouth. He wasn't more than five-nine, but because of his thinness and the stiff way he carried himself, he seemed much taller. Everything about him was plain, and only his boots had cost money. That would be the Army influence, Gatling thought.

"Why did you come down here?" Frobisher asked in a dry, sharp New England voice.

Gatling was surprised—not a lot, but some; he had expected Frobisher to be a little more flamboyant. He didn't expect him to look like a swaggering badman in a tent show, but the very plainness of the man was surprising.

"I came down to talk," Gatling said. "I volunteered to come down. The others are afraid."

Gatling was playing it straight, which might be the only way to convince Frobisher that he wasn't a fake. He had a name and a history ready. He was Albert Burns, originally from Doylestown, Pennsylvania, and had worked at any number of jobs since he was twelve.

But Frobisher asked him none of that. "Why aren't you afraid?"

"Why should you kill me? I'm just a laborer."

It was stinking hot under the trees. Frobisher said, "What's going on up there? They want to give up, is that it? Spell it out for me. You talk and I'll listen. You want a drink of water?"

Frobisher watched while Gatling gulped from a canteen. "All right, you don't have to drink it dry. Water running low up there?"

Gatling said it was. Then he told the rest of his story, keeping it simple because he knew Frobisher would bring him up short if he started to wander.

Frobisher's expression didn't change no matter what Gatling said. Gatling talked in a slow, steady voice, trying to give the impression of an honest, hard-working man, no great brain, but far from dumb. Gatling had known men like that and now, remembering how they sounded, he started to think he might come out of this all right.

It was an easy story to tell because most of it was true. Nothing about Wheeler had to be made up; it was crazy enough to begin with. Gatling told how Wheeler drank from morning till night. He didn't whine, he stated the facts. There was no order, no discipline; some of the engineers were starting to drink as heavily as their boss. The rest of the expedition just wanted to get out.

Gatling said, "I don't know what's between you and Mr. Wheeler, sir. It must be very serious for it to come to shooting. The people I am speaking for do not want to get mixed up in it more than they are. They want to know if you will let them go. They don't care about the expedition any more. They will abandon their instruments, tear up their notebooks if you let them go."

Frobisher stared at Gatling. "Odd they'd send a laborer to talk for them. Well-educated people. You'd think at least one of them would have enough nerve to come down and talk. I'm ready to let them go. I'll even let Wheeler go if he gets out of Panama and never comes back. Let me look at your hands."

"What?"

"Show your hands."

Gatling held out his hands, palms up, and Frobisher inspected them for calluses, old scars, the look of years of hard work. They were not the hands of a convict in a stone quarry, but neither were they the hands of a banker or a professional gambler.

"You're a laborer, all right," Frobisher said. "Or are you a Marine? Not a private at your age. Too old. What are you, a sergeant?"

Gatling didn't even blink. "I'm not one of the Marines," he said. "I don't know much about them. They take their orders from a lieutenant named Mackenzie, who gets his orders from Mr. Wheeler."

Some of Frobisher's men were sitting on a rubber ground
sheet, playing poker for pennies. No whiskey bottles were
around. The men were hard-looking, but without the rummy
craziness often found in killer outfits. Maybe they drank and went
crazy in town, but not here. Frobisher had them under tight
control. His outfit, Gatling thought, was in better shape than
Wheeler's. Naturally the difference was in the men themselves.
Wheeler might have remained a successful self-advertiser,
trading on other men's reputations, if booze hadn't got him.
Booze and some dark side of his nature. But Frobisher was
what he'd been from the beginning, a killer. Nothing about him
helped to explain how he'd gotten that way.

Frobisher had been thinking. Gatling knew he was thinking
about him. He made no attempt to hide it. He was strangely
open in his manner, not friendly or anything even close to it,
just very direct in what he said. Now he looked straight at
Gatling with calm, clear eyes.

"Why didn't you mention the Marines?" he asked. "You
talked about engineers and other technical men, but you didn't
mention that there were Marines out of uniform. Why was that?"

"I didn't think of them as Marines. They've been working
as porters since we left the States."

"They're still Marines. When the sloop *Jackson* left the
Brooklyn Navy Yard there were twenty Marines on board—
two lieutenants, eighteen enlisted men. Everybody on board
knew what they were. So did you. Why didn't you mention
them? Were you told not to?"

"No. Nobody told me to do anything but explain how things
are with us. They are very bad. We have food but we need
water. Some of the men are very sick."

A slight uneasiness showed in Frobisher's eyes. "Fever?"

"They have dysentery," Gatling said. "The doctor is
worried. He wants to try to get them to the French hospital in
Panama City. Others are sick with other ailments. There is one
case of malaria, but the Marine who has it caught it in Louisiana
years ago. There is a lot of worry up there."

"There is a man with a light machine gun up there," Frobisher stated, not just said. "His name is Gatling. That's his real name? You know him as such?"

Gatling said, "I was told his name was Gatling. He's never spoken to me."

"He has the gun?"

"Some sort of gun in a box. But he won't be using it."

"What's that mean? That he's dead."

Gatling said, "He has a bad head wound. One of your bullets hit the rock, then struck him in the head. He has been in a coma, what the doctor calls it, for three days."

"And the machine gun?"

"It's in its box. Nobody knows how to use it, only Gatling. He never taught anybody how to use it."

"*Captain* Frobisher."

"Captain Frobisher, what can I tell them when I go back up there?"

"You're sure you're going back?" The question sounded casual, but Gatling sensed, almost smelled, the immense cruelty behind it. Frobisher could turn vicious at any moment. His plainspoken manner was genuine; it was what lay behind it that made him so sinister.

"I hope you'll let me go back," Gatling said. "You have no reason to harm me. I don't own a gun. I don't know how to use a gun."

Frobisher looked at a mosquito on the back of his hand. It was sucking his blood. He looked at it while Gatling waited for an answer. Finally, Frobisher killed the mosquito, not slapping at it as another man might have, but smearing it with his forefinger. There was blood on his finger and on the back of his hand.

"Here's what you tell them," Frobisher said. "Tell them you are to wave the flag you have in your hand when they're ready to give up. Any guns up there must be brought down and surrendered. We will give you water. If you have food, then you have no need of ours. Everything but food and water must be left behind. Tell them the expedition is finished.''

"How much time do they have to decide?"

"What's there to decide? If they stay up there they'll die. Look—what's your name?—I don't want to kill anybody.''

"My name is Albert Burns," Gatling said. "Albert or Al or just Burns.''

"That's fine, Al. You tell those people up there they have to decide what they want to do. Just don't leave it too long, you tell them. It's not all up to me, you understand.''

"I understand, Mr. Frobisher.''

"Remember, Al, you're to wave the flag when they're ready to give up. If they're in such poor condition, why don't they come down today.''

"I'll tell them that, what you said.'' Frobisher would kill every last one of them if he got the chance. He had them marked for death no matter what they did. They could fight like tigers or slobber over his boots; in the end, it would make no difference.

"Tell them today is the best time to come down," Frobisher urged. "We have more than enough water. Tell them my men will escort them through Urbino's country. Urbino is a rebel, a bandit, very dangerous. They call him El Tigre. You better get back before the day is gone.''

Frobisher called the rifleman who'd brought Gatling in. "Take him out," he said.

Chapter
ELEVEN

"He wasn't surprised by anything I told him," Gatling said. "Mostly he just listened. What I said about the light gun sounded kind of weak, the only man who could use it being out of commission. But I didn't kill myself off. I got hit by a ricochet and I'm in a coma and not likely to come out of it."

"I'm glad you're not dead," O'Sullivan said. "What would we do without you?"

"Maybe he believed me," Gatling said to Mackenzie. "Most of what I told him was the flat truth. Who would need to make up yarns about Wheeler? I think the clincher was the water running out."

"So it is," Mackenzie said. "You think he'll hold off?"

"Most likely. But there's no way to know what he's thinking, or what he'll do. He just listens, doesn't show a thing. Man wasn't even that threatening, doesn't think he has to be. Quiet, well spoken, no bad language, and yet he manages to let you know that he'll do anything."

"So we go ahead with the plan?"

"Such as it is, Mac. He can't know about the Maximite. The Maximite is going to decide it if we get to plant it in the right places and run the fuses back up here. Only chance we have is a dark night."

"I keep thinking about that," Mackenzie said. "There's been too much of a moon. Each night brighter than the one before, God damn it."

"Got to wait, Mac. They'll be watching for anything they can see. I doubt if Frobisher has night glasses, a new thing in the German Army, but who can tell? We have to wait."

O'Sullivan put a fresh cigar in his mouth. "And pray. Better you pray, Mackenzie. I'm an atheist."

Dr. LaPlante came out of Wheeler's cave and crawled toward them. The doctor was a tall man and didn't think bending over was enough. The shooting from below had stopped, at least for now, but he was taking no chances. Gatling liked the doctor even if the doctor didn't like him. The doctor was all right, soured by life and his profession, but a man who wasn't afraid of much, if anything. Maybe he had seen too much death to be afraid of dying.

"You wanted to know how he is," he said. "How he is is not as bad as he was. I'm going to start him on chloral hydrate as soon as the morphia wears off. Don't want him to get too fond of morphia."

"Yes, but will he be all right?" Mackenzie said. "Will he have to be carried when we break out of here?"

"How soon will that be?"

"When there's a dark enough night."

"Very good, Mr. Mackenzie," the doctor said wearily. "Very precise. You tell me when there's a dark enough night and I'll tell you if Wheeler has to be carried."

Mackenzie ignored the sarcasm. The doctor was not a young man, and he was tired. "I'll do that, Doctor."

Nothing could be done that night because the mountain slope was washed in moonlight. Gatling broke out the sticks of Maximite, and collected all the small rocks he could find after he got a roll of sticky tape from Garth, the chief engineer, who wanted to know what he was planning.

"Tape one stick to one rock, then keep on taping till the roll is used up. Fifty sticks should do it, not that we're going to throw fifty sticks at them. Could bring down the side of the mountain, we used that many. Down on them and down on us. Ten sticks ought to be enough. I'll plant charges and run fuses back up here if I can. If I can't, we'll throw it. Be good if we could do both."

Garth looked at the Maximite. "You've had a lot of experience with this stuff?"

"Never used it before, Mr. Garth."

Garth swallowed hard. "Well, if the mountain comes down on us, it'll be better than waiting for Frobisher."

"Anyway, it'll be quick," Gatling said.

He got Mackenzie to help him with the taping, no one else. The Marines were watching the slope, and had their work cut out for them. He didn't trust the civilians to do it right; they were too nervous, and a stick that came loose as it was being thrown could blow them all to bits.

"Who'll do the throwing?" Mackenzie asked.

"You and me," Gatling said. "We'd have a big edge if we could plant the charges. Put them in the right places, we can start a rockslide."

"Maybe tonight. Want me to come with you?"

"Could use the help, but you better stay here. If I don't get to plant the charges . . ."

"You mean if you get killed?"

"If I don't get it done," Gatling said, "you'll have to rely on what we have here."

Mackenzie smiled. "Sticks and stones."

"Get Garth to help you. The important thing is not just driving them off. Frobisher has a lot of men down there. It won't be enough to kill half of them. Leave enough of them alive and you're done for."

"Aye, aye, sir."

"Sorry, Mac. I have a way of telling people what to do."

That night they waited for the moon to come up, and at first there was too much light, but after they waited for three hours, it got cooler and there were clouds, black and ragged and blowing hard. Now and then the moon broke through, but the light didn't last for long.

"I don't know what to think," Mackenzie said.

"It's as good as we're likely to get," Gatling said. "We could wait a week and find nothing better. Anyway, we don't have that much time."

Gatling, his face and hands darkened with dust, moved down the slope, paying out the fuse behind him. For as long as it lasted, the moon was covered by rolling black clouds. For as long as it lasted, he thought. Five minutes, two minutes, no minutes? Up above him, Mackenzie held the wooden spool of fuse, letting it out a few feet. Too much of it might get caught on something. Gatling knew it wouldn't break, but he didn't want to climb back up to free it from a rock or a bush. The fuse was thin and gray and wasn't likely to be spotted even by day. He hoped it wouldn't. He hoped the goddamned moon would stay down.

The dark protected him, but it wasn't easy to see. On the way down to talk to Frobisher, and on the way back, he had noted this and that, but nobody could remember everything. Besides, that had been in glaring sunlight; now it was close to full dark, and some things were not where he expected to find them.

The slope, broken and stepped back in places, was covered with thornbrush and boulders, shale and sand, and there were sudden drops that could kill or cripple a man. Once, the fuse snagged on something, and he had to give it a cautious tug to get it loose.

The slope was long, and he had to go down far to place the charges. He was about halfway there when the clouds cleared the face of the moon, and he felt like a crawling bug under a bright light. There was no thornbush where he was and he lay flat, waiting for a scoped-rifle bullet to plow into him. Frobisher's marksmen had to be the best; they would kill him sure if they got him in their sights. He waited, counting off the seconds.

He was up to 240 when the moon clouded again and he moved on, thinking he'd make better time on the way back. He got to the first place, a shelf of rock with an outthrusting overhang, and he had to climb down one side of it. He had to tug the fuse before he got to the bottom.

The moon broke through again, but for now there was no way they could see him because of the rocks and thornbrush. He pulled a thorn as thick as a sailmaker's needle from the palm of his hand and hoped the wound wouldn't fester. Then he placed the charge, ten sticks of Maximite, and weighted it with rocks. After that he moved along the side of the slope where enormous boulders were piled high and placed the second charge, ten more sticks, and secured it in the same way as the first. If the charge worked right, it would send rocks the size of houses crashing down on top of Frobisher's men.

There were two long waits, while the moon was bright, before he got back to the top. Mackenzie handed him a canteen, and he forced himself not to drink too much. Coming so close to death could make a man thirsty.

He decided not to cut the fuses from the spool until it was time to blow the charges. A night-prowling animal could pull the fuses loose, and then all that work wouldn't be worth shit. Cutting the fuses could be done in seconds.

"I guess we're ready for them," Mackenzie said.

"As we'll ever be," Gatling said. "The only thing is, they'll see the fuses burning if they come by night. They'll see them even with a full moon. By day there'd be too much sun."

"Then we have to hope they come by day."

"They might. It's a long, hard climb to do in the dark. If Frobisher thinks we're too far gone to put up much of a fight, he may take us head-on. He knows we've lost a lot of men, knows our water is about gone. What have we got to stop him? A handful of Marines, a bunch of civilians that know nothing about fighting, a drunken leader. Frobisher has plenty of men, won't mind losing a fair number if it gets the job done. All depends on what he thinks about the light gun. If he thinks I lied, he may just sit down there till we die up here. But I won't use the light gun or the automatic rifle unless they get too close."

"And the mortar?" Gatling had shown the mortar to Mackenzie, explained how it worked. Covered with a rubber groundsheet, it now stood ready, a box of shells beside it.

"We won't use it unless we have to," Gatling repeated. "We're not out of the woods even if we put Frobisher down for good."

"Meaning Urbino's guerrillas? I was hoping maybe we'd get lucky on that score. We haven't seen hide or hair of—what did you call him?—El Tigre and his *insurectos*."

Everybody but the Marine sentries was asleep or pretending to be. No sound came from the cave where the great man lay drugged.

"Maybe we won't," Gatling said. "Could be he's off somewhere, bushwhacking Colombian soldiers, or running from them. But we can't go on that. We have to be ready for the bastard. Right now we're about halfway to the coast. We'll find out for sure between here and there. Frobisher may know something about this shithole of a country, but he can't know it like Urbino—and don't think Urbino's men are armed with a bunch of old muskets and shotguns. DeLesseps gave him the latest French Lebel rifles, hoping to make peace with Urbino. Modern bolt-actions and a sack of money. Urbino used the Lebels against DeLesseps and bought more new rifles with the money."

Mackenzie sighed. "Ah, well, it'll all come out in the wash."

They went over it again, though there was no need to. If Frobisher attacked by day, the remaining Marines would put up a token defense, which in truth was all their single-shot carbines were capable of doing. The civilians would not use their revolvers because the range was too long. Frobisher would understand that. The light gun would not be used even when Frobishber's men started up the slope, dodging from rock to rock, crawling when they had to. The fuses were timed and would not be lit until the attackers had climbed up high, had reached a point from which there was no easy escape, no quick way to get back.

"A," Mackenzie said. "The rock slide may kill every last man without any more help from us. B, if some survive, maybe a lot, and keep coming at us, we let loose with the Maximite

and you open fire with the machine gun. You think we have
to go on to C?''

"Guess not, Mac, but if it comes to C, we'll hit them with
everything in the attic.''

Mackenzie gave another sigh. "Unless, of course, the whole
mountain comes down on us.''

Gatling smiled at him. "Cheer up, Mac. Think of it this way.
At least the wild dogs won't dig us up.''

Gatling and Mackenzie slept for a few hours, but were making
coffee with the last of the water before the civilians crept out
of their blankets. None of them wanted to face another day,
though some put on a better face than others. Gatling didn't
fault the ones who were increasingly afraid. They were out of
their element here; they shouldn't have been here at all. The
whole expedition had been poorly planned, with no concern for
or any real knowledge of what they faced. If they were afraid,
they had a right to be. You had to be trained to fight, but you
had to train yourself to be ready to die.

Sarah Morrison and O'Sullivan crawled over to get their half
cup of coffee.

O'Sullivan raised up to take a quick look down the slope.
"Not a creature is stirring, not even a mouse," he said, easing
his bony backside down on the bare rock.

"Keep your stupid head down or they'll blow it off.''
Mackenzie was angry. "You think they wouldn't? Why
wouldn't they?''

O'Sullivan sipped his coffee, trying to make it last. "I can't
think of a single reason, Mr. Mackenzie.''

Sarah Morrison drank coffee and grimaced. "You didn't have
to wash your socks in it, Gatling. Or was it your drawers?''

"Both. The water was hot, so why not?''

"I'd rather drink plain water than this slop.''

Gatling said, "The water had to be boiled, so we added beans
and got coffee. If you don't want it, give it to O'Sullivan and
he'll drink it.''

O'Sullivan pretended to be alarmed. "What have you got against me? Peace, my children. The enemy is down below. How's that for a pithy observation?"

"Is that what it is?" Mackenzie smiled into his empty cup.

Gatling said, "Here comes the doctor."

Dr. LaPlante made his way over from Wheeler's cave. He had spent the night sitting up with the great man, but it didn't look as if he had slept much. Gatling gave him the rest of the coffee.

"He's coming out of it sooner than I anticipated," the doctor said. "He's as strong as a bull, or was. That helps. I expect to get him on his feet sometime today. On his feet but shaky. What he'll do or say I have no idea, but at least he won't have to be carried. That's what you wanted to know?"

Gatling nodded. "You don't think he'll start acting up? I've seen drunks do that when the craving comes back."

The doctor gave Gatling a cold look. "I've already told you I don't know what he'll do. But since you've asked my opinion, I don't think he will. I suppose you'll have to restrain him if he does, but do it as gently as you can. The sudden shock and rage at being tied like an animal could throw him into convulsions which could prove fatal. But that's not my responsibility anymore. I've got to get some sleep."

Gatling thought, I'll be as easy as I can, as rough as I have to. This was their last chance to get out of this alive, and Wheeler's state of health didn't matter a damn. There would be trouble later if Wheeler died, but later was later.

One of the Marine sentries called out, "They're waving a white flag down there, Mr. Mackenzie. Looks like they want to talk, sir."

Mackenzie told him to keep his head down and keep his eyes on the slope. "They're getting impatient," he said to Gatling.

"Must be so," Gatling said. This could be it or close to it, he thought. Frobisher looked like he had the controlled patience of the professional killer, but every man had his limits. Hot as hell where they were, it was far worse down in the stinking jungle.

Tabor came out of the cave, pale and nervous. After he crawled over he said, "You won't go down and talk to them? What harm can it do?"

Gatling despised Tabor not so much because he was weak but because he was shifty. "It could do harm to me. I already been down. The idea is to bring them up to us. Is Wheeler awake? Did he send you out here?"

Tabor licked his lips, a habit he had. "I'll overlook your insolence because . . . Nobody has to send me. You said yourself Frobisher promised to let us go if we just abandoned everything and went home. So if we go . . . why should he kill us? What would be the point?"

Studying his cigar ash, O'Sullivan laughed to himself.

Gatling wanted to pick Tabor up and throw him down the slope. "The point is, he's that kind of man. If you don't like that point, here's another. We're witnesses, you get that? Even you should be able to get that." Gatling didn't often let his temper loose, but he was close to it now. "The vicious son of a bitch killed a good Marine. If we go home, then he can't, because somebody in the Corps will do something about him and he knows it. The crawling scum wants us all dead—and so do the people who hired him. Now you go back and tell the great man that's the straight of it."

"No need to tell me anything." They all turned when Wheeler walked out of the cave like a ham actor making a stage entrance. All he had on was an undershirt and torn trousers, wet with sweat—no boots—and his big body seemed to be melting like a wax figure left too long in the sun.

O'Sullivan's emaciated body shook with silent laughter. No one else found it funny.

Tabor tried to tell him to get down. "Dock . . . Mr. Wheeler . . ."

Wheeler snapped his fingers and Tabor shut up. A sudden mad rage took hold of Wheeler and spent spasms through his entire body. He pointed at Gatling and shouted, "Damn you! God damn you! How dare you try to take over here?" Gobs of spit flew from his mouth. His mouth was trembling. "I am

Murdock Johnson Wheeler. I am . . . I will make the decisions!
I will deal with Frobisher! I will accept Frobisher's offer, but
who is the better man? He will find himself tricked and out-
maneuvered . . . I will . . . I will go down there *now* . . .''

A bullet hit the rock close to Wheeler's head and he stood
there trembling. "Frobisher . . . as one man to another . . .''
he was saying.

Gatling and Mackenzie brought him down hard. He was big
and heavy and it took both of them to do it. Mackenzie, red-
faced, yelling, told two Marines to gag and bind him.

"They're starting up, Mr. Mackenzie," a corporal sang out.

Wheeler was struggling with the two Marines. Mackenzie
roared, "Get it done! Get it finished! Get back to your posts!
Open fire, you mothers' sons . . .''

The Marines were firing down the slope from behind the
broken natural rock wall. Wheeler lay on his back, his hands
tied in front of him, with the doctor kneeling beside him to
remove the gag from his mouth. Gatling moved the binoculars,
looking for Frobisher and not finding him, and while he was
still looking a Marine took a bullet in the face and died. Next
to Gatling, Mackenzie was firing steadily with a Springfield
carbine. The fire from below was fierce, heavy, concentrated,
and fast, but they were firing uphill, not the best way to shoot.
Still, they were firing for effect more than anything else. It
sounded as if a small army was attacking. Still looking for
Frobisher, Gatling estimated there were 50 or 60 men coming
up through the rocks and thornbrush. Now they had cleared the
bottom of the slope and were on the slope itself, dodging and
crawling, and in places having to climb, but so far they hadn't
reached the point he had set for them in his mind. The fuses
were timed, and he counted as he watched the crawling and
climbing men through the glasses. He had a cigar in his mouth,
and so did Mackenzie, and he knew Frobisher's men hadn't
seen anything that would make them stop and try to go back.

No one else was hit because the uphill shooting wasn't
accurate. Maybe the dead Marine had been killed by a stray
bullet. Then Gatling changed his mind. Maybe the bullet had

been fired by a sharpshooter who wasn't part of the attack. That was something to think about, because if there were sharpshooters shooting at them from the edge of the jungle where they couldn't be killed by the rockslide he hoped to send down on them, that was bad. They would have to deal with the sharpshooters later if they could.

Looking through the glasses, he saw no casualties down there. But there was no way to tell, unless a man hit by a bullet jumped or lurched or threw up his arms, or did something else that showed that he had been hit. Mackenzie was still firing, and so were the Marines. The civilians were crouched behind the shield of broken rock, clutching their revolvers and waiting for the order to open fire, not knowing that they wouldn't be ordered to do anything unless the charges failed to explode or unless the charges failed to stop the attack.

Gatling stopped counting and set the binoculars down. The first of the attackers had reached the point he had decided on, and the others were coming up fast behind them. Mackenzie turned as Gatling reached over to slap him on the shoulder. Gatling touched off the two long fuses, and Mackenzie smiled like a devil, though there was nothing devilish about him. The fuses caught and burned and hissed away from them, went out through the rocks and down the slope. Heavy fire was still coming at them from the slope and the Marines were firing back, and Gatling started his final count. Behind him, no longer gagged, Wheeler was roaring in mad, futile anger, and even with all that was going on, the crash of rifles and the whine of bullets, the doctor was urging him to be calm.

Gatling continued to count. . . .

The side of the mountain shook as the charges exploded, and right on top of the first tremor came a deeper rumbling, and from up above small rocks rained down on them, and immediately after that the entire slope below them began to move and fall away from the mountain itself, and even at a distance Gatling heard Frobisher's men screaming as the world fell in on them.

The rumbling went on and then it stopped, and it was a while before Gatling was able to see anything because of the dust cloud that boiled up. Even when he wiped dust from the lenses of the binoculars, it was still hard to pick up anything. The automatic rifle and the light gun and the rest of the Maximite stood ready, but he knew he wouldn't have to use anything else, at least not here.

Suddenly there wasn't a sound. The last rock rolled down and stopped, and when it did everything was quiet. As he stood up he heard Mackenzie telling the civilians to stay where they were. Mackenzie looked over at Gatling and smiled, no longer devilish but satisfied that they had done all right. Gatling wiped the lenses again and looked down the slope, and saw nothing but the little mountain made by the rockslide. The side of the mountain had dropped right off from under where they were, and it was nothing but chance that had kept them from going along with it.

He moved the binoculars, still looking for Frobisher or anything, any sign of life, even a dying man. No bullets came at them, but that didn't mean Frobisher and his best sharp-shooters, maybe two or three, weren't down there under the cover of the trees.

He'd done all right, but he would have liked to see Frobisher's dead body—even better if he had killed the bastard himself—and he felt a bit let down when the civilians, thinking they were out of it, gave him a hip-hip-hooray. The civilians were jaunty now, and even boastful, still brandishing their revolvers and telling each other the terrible things they would have done to Frobisher, the blackguard, if he had been unlucky enough to get close to their diggings.

Mackenzie and his men had gone down to look for signs of life in the rubble of the mountain, and when they returned and said there was nothing alive down there, the civilians cheered them too. They hadn't been shot at, and now O'Sullivan and his assistant, Bigelow, were disappointed because there was nothing to photograph but rocks.

There was fresh water now, and everybody was cheerful.

Mackenzie told Gatling he had found nothing but supplies and water in Frobisher's jungle camp.

"We explored the jungle a bit," Mackenzie said. "But nobody went out by the back door, no sign that anybody did. I counted the groundsheets, the best I could tell you how many men had been there. My figure is fifty-eight. There could've been that many men coming up at us. My figures tally with yours?"

"More or less," Gatling said.

Chapter
TWELVE

By nightfall they were five miles from where most of them had expected to die. They could have made better time if not for Wheeler, who couldn't move very fast. But at least he didn't have to be carried and he gave no trouble, not even when they abandoned everything they didn't need. After talking to Gatling, Mackenzie told Garth his people could keep anything they could carry themselves, but that his men would do no more useless donkey work. Everybody had to pitch in, no argument about it.

Nobody argued; they just wanted to get the hell home.

One of the first things abandoned was Sarah Morrison's enormous typewriter. She didn't want to carry it; nobody offered to do it for her. It hardly mattered; the machine was starting to rot.

They picked up the Mono River and followed it southwest. No more Indians, no more poisoned arrows. But a heavy guard was posted when they made camp for the night.

Camp was a patch of high, dry ground far back from the river, on the edge of the wide savannah covered with dry yellow grass that waved in the hot wind. The hill gave them an advantage; they could see for miles in all directions.

There was no shortage of food and water. Mackenzie's men had taken Frobisher's food and water, and there was river water,

boiled for a long time to make it safe. Gatling knew Sarah
Morrison still had some liquor, and he warned her not to let
Wheeler get at it.

"No need to worry," she said. "It's too precious to me."

Wheeler was like a man in a dream, quiet but dazed, and
Gatling wondered if the man had lost his mind or had been a
little crazy to begin with. It was no skin off his ass what Wheeler
was as long as he didn't give any trouble. He was being paid
to protect the son of a bitch, and he would protect him and do
his damnedest to get him home.

With the tents set up, it wasn't so bad, and smoke from the
cook fires helped to keep the mosquitoes at bay; away from the
smoke, you were bitten bloody. Thanks to quinine, nobody had
come down with malaria, which could kill you if you got it bad
enough, and there was no recurrence of yellow fever.

Fritz set up Wheeler's tent as soon as they made camp. Now
it was dark, and Wheeler was in his tent lying on his cot while
Fritz cooked some kind of stew. When it was ready Irby took
it into the tent.

Gatling, Mackenzie, Sarah Morrison, O'Sullivan, and his
assistant, Bigelow, ate supper together. Sarah Morrison cooked
it. It was the first time Gatling had seen her cook anything.
Usually she and Olds, the newspaperman, took their meals with
Garth and his people. Olds was with them now.

"What is it?" O'Sullivan asked her when he tasted what was
on his plate.

Sarah Morrison was looking at Bigelow, a man of about 22,
quiet and inclined to be bashful. He wasn't tall but he was
powerfully built, and he had been O'Sullivan's assistant for four
years. He wore his hair in a stiff Prussian cut.

"It's bully beef stew," she said absently. "With dried
potatoes, rice, onion powder, salt and pepper."

"So that's what happened to the horse," O'Sullivan said.

The others ate their food without comment. Too much salt
but nobody cared. It was some kind of food and they could eat
it without being shot at. At most, they were about three days
from Panama City.

Mackenzie said to Gatling, "It's not going so badly so far. How does it look to you?"

Gatling was glad to be drinking real coffee. "Looks like what I can see, Mac."

Gatling knew Mackenzie was just making talk because he was embarrassed by the way Sarah Morrison was looking at young Bigelow. Now that she thought she was out of the woods, she was acting uppity again. That was how she was, up or down, frightened or arrogant, depending on how things were at the moment. The passing of danger seemed to make her randy, as he well knew. He wondered why she didn't pick on one of the engineers, surveyors, or mapmakers. She had used up some of them on the ship, one or two since leaving it; maybe she thought it was time for a change.

O'Sullivan didn't miss it either; he'd have to be blind if he did, Gatling thought. For his part, he didn't care one way or another. None of his business unless it made trouble. If she wanted to take a crack at Bigelow, why not? She could hardly hold her Ivor Johnson revolver to the poor fellow's head, and from the way Bigelow was taking it, it didn't look as if she'd have to.

But O'Sullivan didn't like it. Suddenly he said to Bigelow, "I'll bet the wife and kids'll be glad to have you home, Eddie."

Bigelow was startled. Gatling knew he wasn't married. Bigelow was so flustered he didn't know what to say. In the end, all he managed to do was give a short, nervous laugh, then bend his head over his plate.

Sarah Morrison gave O'Sullivan a dirty look. "Too bad you don't have a wife and kiddies, Tim. That'd keep you too busy to be sticking your nose in other people's affairs."

"Ah, you know how I am, Sarah. If I can't have Lily Langtry, I don't want anybody."

"Who would want you?" She tried to make a joke out of it by laughing. There was an awkward pause, and then she started to say something to Bigelow.

O'Sullivan stood up. "Time to get some sleep, Eddie. Mr. Mackenzie here will be cracking the whip at first light, isn't that right?''

Mackenzie didn't answer; he was annoyed at being used as an excuse. Gatling didn't blame him. He was good and sick of all these people; the only one he wouldn't be glad to see the last of was Mackenzie. The others seemed to be driven by things he could only guess at, if he felt like guessing. Fine if he met O'Sullivan or Sarah at some other time, in some other place. For now they grated on his nerves.

Mackenzie said he had to see how the guards were doing. Gatling was left with Sarah Morrison, who took out her flask, unscrewed the top, and poured brandy in her coffee. She shook the flask at Gatling. ''Want some?''

Gatling said no thanks.

''It makes me feel better,'' she said. ''Don't you ever get drunk?''

''Now and then. Only when I feel like it. I don't want to get drunk here.''

''Meaning you don't want to get drunk with me?''

''You or anybody.''

She belted back the spiked coffee. ''Lawd a mussy! What would we-all do if you was to git dronk?''

''I thought you said liquor made you feel better.''

''It does make me feel better,'' she said defiantly. ''Don't you think I sound like it's making me feel better?''

Gatling said no.

She drank the next drink, a much bigger drink, without coffee. Then she started in again. ''You know, it must be wonderful to be so strong and self-sufficient. No self-doubts, no moments of indecision. You're so wonderful it's a wonder you can stand yourself.''

Gatling said he had to try hard.

That got to her. She lost her temper. ''I don't think you're so wonderful. In fact, I don't think you're wonderful at all. I think you're a two-faced, hypocritical son of a bitch like O'Sullivan. It's all right for a man to have all the women he wants, but when a woman . . .''

She paused to drink and Gatling said, ''I wouldn't mind it

if you stopped laying into me. I'm not the hero of this place.
If you want to spread your legs for that kid, go right to it. Just
don't be making trouble. In a few days, if we're lucky, we'll
be . . .''

She got up so fast she nearly lurched into the fire. Seeing
her mad and half drunk or whole drunk was nothing new. He
didn't care.

''We'll be where I won't have to look at your ugly face
again,'' she said, then walked away to her tent.

Starting out at dawn, they made nine miles the next day. They
followed the river, and there were two 20-minute rests when
they chewed hardtack and drank water. Watched over by Irby
and Fritz, Wheeler gave no trouble; he even showed some
interest in his surroundings, but said nothing. It stayed quiet
all day, and the only part of it Gatling didn't like was when
they had to drive off crocodiles with rifle fire. But there was
no help for it: the three monsters came charging out of the
muddy shallows.

During the early afternoon they got all the way through the
river gap in the last straggle of mountains. They weren't up
high enough to see the Bay of Panama, but it was dead ahead,
no more than 15 or 20 miles away, and when they reached it
they would follow the coast down to Panama City.

That night they camped far back from the river; at their backs
were low brown hills covered with brush and stunted trees. Not
the best location for a camp, but it was getting dark and everybody was tired. They got the tents up and the cook fires started.
Mackenzie came to eat with Gatling and O'Sullivan after he
posted the guard. Sarah Morrison was over with the engineers;
there was a lot of laughing.

Tonight O'Sullivan did the cooking: salt bacon and beans,
with canned peaches for dessert. ''Better than the truck her
ladyship dished up last night,'' O'Sullivan said. ''Not much you
can do to wreck bacon and beans.''

Mackenzie chewed on the undercooked bacon. ''You made
a pretty good try.''

"At least Eddie likes my cooking. Look at the way that boy is shoveling it in."

Bigelow had all but cleared his plate; averting his eyes, he said he was tired out and wanted to get some sleep. Taking his plate with him, he walked away before O'Sullivan could say anything else.

"A good lad," O'Sullivan said. "Someday he's going to make a fine photographer."

They worked their way through the peaches. Mackenzie was saying that the first thing he planned to do when they got aboard ship was to take the longest, hottest bath of his life.

"I must stink as bad as you two," he said.

"What's a little stink between friends?" O'Sullivan said. "A cold beer, a hot bath—what more could a man ask for?"

It got late while they talked about cold beer, hot baths, clean clothes, long hours of untroubled sleep. O'Sullivan yawned while he talked, and finally he said he was going to turn in. Gatling and Mackenzie were about to do the same when O'Sullivan came back looking agitated, which wasn't like him.

"Eddie's not in the tent," he said. "And he's not in the . . . she's not there either."

Gatling and Mackenzie got up fast. Gatling told the Irishman to keep his voice down. "They must be out there somewhere, stupid bastards. You stay here. We'll take a look. I said stay here."

After a quick search of the camp they went to question the guards, and found one of them asleep, his chin on his chest, his back against a tree. Mackenzie kicked him awake, and he scrambled to his feet and stood there bewildered and trembling.

"Shut your goddamned mouth," Mackenzie growled when he started to say how sorry he was. "Stay awake or I'll peel the hide off you, and don't shoot us when we come back in."

They found Bigelow's body about a hundred feet from where he and Sarah Morrison had slipped past the sentry. His pants were down and his throat had been cut. There was no sign of the woman. Under the trees it was so dark that it was impossible to see any kind of tracks. All they could do was return to camp, carrying Bigelow's body between them.

Back there they put the body in O'Sullivan's tent after he looked at the dead man, with no expression on his face. "He would have been a fine photographer," was all the Irishman said. Then his face twisted and he added, "That bitch!"

Mackenzie gestured toward the tents where Wheeler and his people were sleeping. "No point waking them at this hour, you agree? If they—whoever they are—planned to attack, they would have done it by now. They know about your weapons. They have to know."

"Probably they know," Gatling said. "All we can do is put out the fires and wait for light."

Gatling looked at the light gun and the mortar, then covered them again. There was plenty of Maximite left. If an attack came, Mackenzie would fire the light gun, Gatling would use the mortar. There were about four hours of darkness left, long enough for anything to happen. The rest of the camp slept on; no sounds came from Wheeler's tent.

The night was hot and thick with bugs and mosquitoes; the stink of the river was heavy on the air.

"You think it's Urbino?" Mackenzie said.

"Could be," Gatling said. "But it doesn't have to be. Panama's crawling with bandits. It could be anybody."

"But not Frobisher? There was no sign of him during the attack."

"It could be Frobisher," Gatling said. "He could be down to a few men. He could be down to himself. If he is, that could explain what happened tonight. Frobisher's the kind of man doesn't give up. Professional pride."

"Some kind of ransom, you think?"

"It could be that. That's what it has to be, unless it's some skulker that wants a good-looking white woman for himself. If that's what it is, then goodbye Sarah. She'll be gone where we could never find her. I don't know that I want to look."

"Ah, Christ! We have to look," Mackenzie said. "She's one of us. What she did was willful and stupid, but still and all . . ."

"We'll look for her," Gatling said. "We'll make a reasonable search, but fair is fair. We had to knock down Wheeler because he was a threat to everybody including himself. Sarah can't be any different."

Mackenzie slapped at a mosquito on the side of his neck. "You're an awful hard man, Gatling. I thought maybe because . . ."

"You thought wrong, Mac. Just because we had a few rolls in the hay doesn't mean I'm going to risk the lives of everyone in this party. A reasonable search, and that's it. If we don't find her, we'll have to move on. She's a full-grown woman even if she doesn't act like one."

Neither man said anything for a while. It was quiet except for some night-hunting animals snuffling in the brush. The sky was clear except for a few clouds idling before a light wind.

"They must have come up real quiet not to be heard," Mackenzie said at last.

Gatling said, "No way it could have been planned. No way they could have known in advance. We didn't, they didn't. Maybe who did it came to grab Sarah, not to stage an attack. She just made it easy, is all. The bastards may have waited till Bigelow was in the saddle before they cut his throat."

"Poor son of a bitch! Ah, but you can't blame the woman. Men and women do these things, the way of human nature. It's not all love in a cottage."

"Nobody's laying blame, Mac," Gatling said. "It's over and done. Least it's over for the kid."

What Gatling thought but didn't say was, "And maybe it's over for us."

The morning sun was hot and bright when one of the guards yelled that two men were coming in under a white flag. By then the others had been told about Bigelow's death and Sarah's disappearance. Not all the civilians—among them men who had shared her bed—wanted to go looking for her. But they knew Mackenzie's order was backed by Gatling's weapons, so they didn't put forward any objections. Now, with two men coming in to talk, they didn't know what to think.

Gatling and Mackenzie stood with the sentry who had given
the alarm. The sentry asked Mackenzie if he should fire a
warning shot. Mackenzie said no, let them come ahead. Gatling
had folded back the bipod of the light gun and carried the weapon
like a heavy rifle.

Mackenzie was using binoculars to get a better look at the
two men approaching the camp. "One man looks like an
American," he said. "The other is a colored man, some kind
of colored. Take a look."

Holding the light gun with one hand, Gatling looked through
the glasses and saw Frobisher. Frobisher appeared to be
unarmed, and he stumbled and nearly fell when the colored man
behind him gave a hard shove. The colored man had a pistol
in his left hand, another pistol in his belt, a rifle slung across
his back. The binoculars brought his face up close: He was
grinning.

"The white one is Frobisher," he told Mackenzie. "He's
coming in under the gun, but maybe he's giving the orders."

They waited for Frobisher and the colored man to get closer.
A lot of ground had to be crossed; it took some time. Blueflies
buzzed in the hot, still air; a big, bright bird perched on a branch
and scolded them.

"Stop right there," Mackenzie called out when Frobisher and
the other man were 25 feet away. "You—whoever you are—
put the gun away and then we'll talk—maybe."

For an instant Gatling thought the colored man was about to
start blasting, it took him so long to stick the long-barreled,
nickel-plated Colt .45 single-action in his belt. He did it slowly,
and he sneered to show them that he wasn't afraid of anything.
Then he laughed a mirthless basso laugh; he laughed so hard
his big body shook. He was very big and very black. He was
handsome and he knew it.

"Whoever I am," he said in a chesty, rumbling voice.
"Whoever I am is Urbino. I am Urbino. I am El Tigre."
Mackenzie's *whoever you are* had offended him and he wanted
them to know it. "I have your woman and I have come to talk."

"Then talk," Mackenzie said.

"First, I expect to be offered the hospitality of your camp." Urbino spoke British island-English flavored with a slight Spanish accent. His parents had come to Panama from Trinidad, Gatling recalled the colonel saying. Beside Urbino, Frobisher stood like a whipped dog. Subservient now because he had to be, Gatling thought, but still a vicious son of a bitch. The blood on his shirt hadn't dried because he was sweating so hard. Gatling figured he had been strung up and flogged.

"No camp," Mackenzie said. "Come in closer. We'll talk here."

Urbino pushed Frobisher ahead of him, then jerked him to a halt. His broad smile was heavy with contempt. "You are Mackenzie and you are Gatling," he said, pointing. "See, I know everything. Our friend here"—he slapped the back of Frobisher's head—"has told me everything. Our friend here came looking for me and, as you can see, he found me. We can do business together, he said. I would be highly rewarded if I helped him to wipe you out. Our friend here said you had a new machine gun, the latest weapon, that was worth its weight in gold. Is that it?"

Gatling had the light gun at his hip, its muzzle pointing directly at Urbino's chest. "This is it," he said.

"And such explosives our friend here told me about." Urbino's big teeth were so white they looked as if they were made of porcelain. "With this latest machine gun and this wonderful explosive I would be the terror of my enemies. What other latest weapons do you want to trade for the woman? You are the weapons expert, Gatling. I am talking to you."

"You're wasting your time," Gatling said. "I won't trade weapons for anything."

Urbino's smile got wider. "Not even for such a beautiful woman? You will agree she is very beautiful. So beautiful, in fact, that I hate to give her up. Such a woman! Such spunk! I can't help but admire her. I will be truthful now and admit that I have done much more than admire her. What a night last night was!"

Mackenzie's sunburned face got redder. "Listen here you—"

"Let him talk," Gatling cut in. "That's what he came for."

Urbino boomed out his big laugh. "Indeed I did. We have begun to talk, so now let us talk some more. That is how business is conducted. I have enjoyed the lady's favors, but my poor men, so long in the womanless jungle, have not yet had the opportunity. There is just so much even I can do to hold them back, if you get my meaning. Some of my men, I must confess, are filthy, unwashed savages, the result of many years of imperialist repression and brutality. Men treated savagely become savages, poor fellows."

"No deal," Gatling said.

"Some of my men are jungle Indians," Urbino went on, still smiling, enjoying the sound of his own voice. He spoke in a rolling, booming voice, and Gatling wondered if his father had been a backcountry preacher in Trinidad. "No Indians more savage than the Panama Indians. So seldom have they seen a white woman, it would be only natural for them to take your beautiful lady back to their village. Of course, her life, when they finally tired of her, would be absolutely unbearable. What happens to her is entirely up to you."

Gatling pretended to whisper something to Mackenzie. Mackenzie nodded several times, and Gatling turned back to Urbino.

"How do we know she's still alive?"

Urbino laughed at such a foolish question. "Would I kill one so lovely?" Then he turned stern. "Of course she's alive. What would I have to trade if she were dead?"

"Then show her," Gatling said. "No more talk till we see her. Is she here now?"

Urbino put on a sly face. "She could be watching us from the trees. She could be many miles away praying that her fine *white* American friends will do something to free her. Let us go into your camp and discuss the matter further. It is hot talking in the sun."

"We'll talk here," Gatling said. Urbino wanted to see if there were other weapons that Frobisher didn't know about. Far from bright, this so-called tiger was conceited, tetchy, unstable—a dangerous combination. "What about the woman? Do we get to see her? There's no point going on with this until we see her."

Urbino pulled his earlobe in a pretense of thought. "You may see her, but not today. She must be brought here from our camp, and so she shall. Does that suit you? Very well. Now let us continue to dicker. My terms are: all your weapons, all your weapons old and new, in exchange for the woman. All weapons includes the machine gun you are pointing at me. Nothing must be hidden, nothing must be left out. It will be very bad for you if you try to trick me."

"So you say. Why don't you just take the weapons? Anyway, try to take them? When you took the woman you could have attacked our camp. Why didn't you?"

Urbino rolled his eyes, the smart rogue who was smarter than any white man. He started his laugh by saying, "Aha, aha," then cut loose with his full basso. He winked at Gatling, one slick rogue sharing a joke with another slick rogue, except that he was slicker than anybody.

"Well you know, Gatling, I am not a fool," he said. "I see the latest machine gun you are pointing at me. What if you have other latest weapons in your camp? Our friend here"—Frobisher cringed as Urbino raised his hand—"seems to think perhaps you do. To attack your camp, with the possibility of such weapons, would be foolhardy. I have many men, but I need all of them. Now, of course, there is no need for any attack."

"Because you have the woman?"

"Because I have the woman. Now the question remains: Do we have a deal or not? The time for dickering is over and you must answer yes or no."

"Not so fast," Gatling said. "You'll get the guns when we get the woman. But we must have safe passage to the coast. You can't have any interest in killing us once you get the guns."

Urbino smiled complacently. "No interest whatsoever. My mission is to liberate Panama, not to kill Americans. But now I must inspect the other weapons. I insist."

Gatling shook his head. "Not before you deliver the woman. How soon will that be?"

Urbino forgot that he had just given his word to be a fair-minded fellow; the look he gave Gatling was expected to make Gatling shake in his boots. Then he remembered, and gave them the full force of his porcelain smile. He had these two white men by the balls, the stupid bastards, and he would deal with their insolence the moment they handed over their weapons.

"At noon tomorrow," he said. "You will see the woman then. Have the weapons ready, and remember this, I will know it if you try to trick me. And then you will all die screaming."

Urbino half turned and pointed to the trees on the far side of the long stretch of open ground. "At this moment a hundred rifles are aimed at you. You may shoot me as I leave, but you will die with me. Our friend here I give you as a gift. You will have plans for him, I am sure."

They watched Urbino until they couldn't see him anymore, then they went back into camp with Frobisher staggering ahead of them. Once he turned and tried to say something. Gatling told him to shut up. Looking at the back of Frobisher's head, he wanted to put a bullet in it. He knew he would kill Frobisher—no matter what else happened, he would kill the son of a bitch—but not before he was through with him. Frobisher had a lot of questions to answer, a lot of talking to do.

He didn't think torture would be necessary.

Chapter
THIRTEEN

They let the doctor see to Frobisher's lacerated back before they sat him down for some hard questioning. The doctor said there was some danger of serious infection, but he didn't seem to be too concerned about it.

They gave Frobisher a fairly clean shirt to cover the bandages. He asked for a cup of coffee, and he got that too. A Marine was posted outside Mackenzie's tent with orders to keep everybody out. Tabor, probably sent by Irby, tried to get in on the interrogation. Mackenzie ordered him to go and check the sentries.

"I can find his camp for you," Frobisher said. "All that country back there looks the same, but I think I can lead you to his camp."

"Sure you can," Gatling said. "Is that Urbino's idea or is it yours?"

Frobisher's hand trembled as he raised the coffee mug to his mouth. "Why do you say that? You saw my back. That nigger bastard had me flogged."

"Good for him," Mackenzie said. "You're worse than any nigger. You're the real nigger bastard here. The hell with your lousy back! A man like you would take a flogging to make it look good for later."

Gatling said, "What's wrong with your story is why would an old hand like you trust the likes of Urbino. What did you hope to gain when you went looking for him?"

Frobisher managed to drink some coffee. "To finish what I started. I thought telling him about your weapons would get me on his good side. Promising to bring him more new guns from the coast was to be my insurance. That nigger is hungry for guns."

"Not a bad idea," Gatling said. "What happened? What went wrong?"

Frobisher touched his battered mouth with one finger. "I don't know what happened. He just turned on me and started slapping my face, then kicking and punching, and then flogging. Said he didn't want to help any stinking white man. He hates whites. Said he'd kick every white man out of Panama when he took over. Any white that tried to stay would be slaughtered."

"You put him on to the woman?" Gatling wanted to throw Frobisher down and kick him in the face. "That was your idea?"

Gatling raised his hand to slap at a mosquito, but Frobisher thought it was being raised to hit him, and he cringed away from it.

"Answer the question," Mackenzie growled.

"That was my idea," Frobisher said. "After I told him about the Maxim gun and said maybe you had other weapons, he didn't want to take you head-on. That's when I suggested taking the woman. He liked the idea. He didn't turn mean till later. When he did, he said no white man could be trusted to keep his word about anything. I would never bring him any guns from the coast. I was no use to him. I was a piece of shit. He beat and kicked me, had me flogged."

"A man of good taste," Mackenzie said. "And now we're expected to believe he turned you over to us as a gesture of good faith?"

"He said I would be a bonus. He said you would know what to do with me."

"So we do." Mackenzie turned to Gatling. "What do you think?"

"I think that's probably what Urbino said. And I'll bet Frobisher here can find his camp without the least bit of trouble. Isn't that right, Frobisher?"

"I never said that. Finding it won't be easy if that's what you have a mind to do. But I made note of things."

Mackenzie was furious. "You didn't rip off pieces of your dress and leave them on thornbushes, did you? Like frontier women did in the Indian captive tales? You didn't mark a trail with a bucket of whitewash and a brush? Or anything of that nature?"

"You can laugh at me if you like. I'm telling you the truth."

Mackenzie told Frobisher to shut his mouth or have it shut for him. Shut up and sewed up.

Frobisher watched in sullen silence as they talked. They talked as if he wasn't there. Nothing he heard would do him any good or them any harm.

"I don't know what to think," Mackenzie said. "The way I see it, the bastard is doing Urbino's dirty work without knowing he's doing it. Or he knows it, sort of knows it, but will play along with anything to stay alive."

Gatling looked at Frobisher, dirty, miserable, beaten down. "That's about the size of it, Mac. Try this on for size. Urbino is very wary of our weapons. He knows we have the Maxim light gun because he's seen it. What else we have he can only guess at."

"He'd shit his pants if he saw the mortar."

"He wants to believe we have weapons could make him king of Panama. He's afraid to take us head-on, but he lusts after those magic weapons. What does that add up to in your book?"

"An ambush?" Mackenzie said quickly. "He's trying to set up an ambush. Walk us into a trap and hit us from all sides. A trap so tight we won't be able to make the best use of our magic weapons."

Frobisher was listening to all this with cabbage ears, as O'Sullivan liked to say.

"That has to be it," Gatling said. "Unless we're way off the mark, Urbino's plan is this. Frobisher helps us to find

Urbino's camp and we hit it hard with everything we've got. Before he has a chance to hit us. We come barreling in expecting to find everybody asleep or at least not ready for a fight. We wipe them out, rescue the maiden from the dragon, and are off to the races. Except they'll be all set and waiting.''

''The big bastard isn't so dumb.''

''Smart in some ways, dumb in others. He'd take Panama a lot sooner if his vanity didn't keep stepping on his dick. Just this once he wants us to think he's a dumb nigger. The hell with caution, he wants us to think. We can run right over this dumb nigger because we're white. What's there to be afraid of? No nigger, the smartest nigger ever was, can make a plan that works.''

Mackenzie sleeved sweat from his face; he looked tired. ''It's all so complicated. Give me a nice simple war any day of the week.'' Then, suddenly frowning, he said, ''Yes, but if we don't go in with guns blazing, what do we do?''

''Creep up on them after we take care of the watchers along the trail. They'll be there, all right, waiting to run and give the alarm when they see us coming. We have to make sure they don't run anywhere.''

''That's a pretty tall order,'' Mackenzie said, looking doubtful.

''So it is,'' Gatling agreed. ''But it's what we have to do. If we don't, then it's goodbye Sarah, and probably goodbye us.''

Gatling knew the first watcher he had to kill would be close to camp, right at the edge of the trees. About 500 yards of open ground covered with savannah grass lay between the camp and where the trees began. It wasn't quite jungle there because the tall trees grew far apart, and between them there was brush instead of creepers and wildly growing plants. He knew they could make good time in there once they got going, but they couldn't wait for night before they started out. There wasn't enough time to wait for darkness. Too much ground had to be covered before the sun went down.

''Have everybody ready,'' he told Mackenzie. ''Build up the

cook fires so there's a lot of smoke. Irby is to remain here with Wheeler. The doctor can do as he pleases.''

"He's coming with us. Wheeler wants to come. I told him no. He seems to be getting better, but I doubt if he's up to this sort of thing.''

They turned as Wheeler and Irby walked up behind them. Wheeler was pale, had lost weight, but his voice was strong enough. "I heard what you just said, Mr. Mackenzie, and you're wrong. Forget our past differences if you can. This isn't the place to discuss them. I want to do just one thing right before this damned thing is over. I'm sober because there isn't anything to drink and isn't likely to be. I'm not saying I'll never drink again, but today I'm cold sober and in fair shape and you need all the men you can get. I used to be a hell of a good shot.''

Mackenzie looked at Gatling. "Come along then," Gatling said. "But this time you'll get more than a rope and a gag if you make trouble.''

Wheeler nodded. "Fair enough. Irb's as good a shot as I am.''

"Fine. Good," Gatling said. "Everybody come along.'' There was one hell of a difference between shooting ducks and shooting men, which is what he figured Wheeler meant when he talked about shooting. What the hell! The worst part of this would be killing Urbino's trail-watchers, and Wheeler and Irby would have no part in that. As far as he knew, there were no saloons in this corner of Panama.

Mackenzie and the two men went to talk to the doctor about giving Wheeler back his weapons; the doctor had impounded them. On his way to the doctor's tent, Mackenzie stopped and told his men to build up the cook fires. Gatling waited while that was being done, then when the camp area was thick with smoke, he edged his way through the tents to the river side of the camp and started to crawl through the savannah grass that grew in close on all sides.

He figured that Mackenzie had seen him go, and that was the way he wanted it. It was going to be a long roundabout crawl, and there could be snakes on the way, but it was the only hope he had of coming up on the trail-watcher without being seen. There could be two watchers, there could be three. He had the Colt .45, hammer thonged in its holster, and the double-edged knife in his boot, but he wouldn't use the Colt unless he had to. Just one shot would send the next trail-watcher running for Urbino's camp. It had to be done with the knife.

He had to crawl through the tall dry yellow grass before he reached the trees. Once he had to raise his head to get his bearings. The camp, on high ground, was wreathed in smoke, and he hoped the watcher or watchers wouldn't decide they were getting ready to move out. It was hot as hell in the dry grass, and bugs and flies drew blood from his face and hands. He killed an evil-looking spider that was fixing to bite through his shirt. When he got into the cover of the trees he was soaked in sweat and thinking of a mug of cold beer.

He dodged from tree to tree, his boots making no sound in the thick carpet of rotting vegetation. Birds with bright plumage squawked and flew away from him, and after that it was dead quiet. A hot wind rustled the branches of the trees, but that was the only sound. Then he heard them, two men, talking; there could be a third man who had nothing to say.

There was no third man. Two men squatted at the edge of the trees, their Lebel bolt-action rifles across their thighs, and their backs were turned and they were talking in Spanish. They passed a bottle while they talked. They were half-castes, and they were dressed in dirty white cotton, loose pants, and shirt, the pants held up by drawstrings, and big floppy hats to keep off the sun. The bottle was about half gone; he was close enough to see it was half empty, and it showed in the way they talked and sometimes laughed.

Gatling crept closer. One of the men began to sing softly, humming in the places where he didn't know the words. It must have been a dirty song or a funny song, because the other man laughed at the words. Gatling sprang forward and smashed the singer across the head with the barrel of the Colt, and the other man yelled and started to fumble with his rifle bolt. He was still yelling and fumbling when Gatling crashed down on him and buried the double-edged knife in his heart.

Gatling killed the singer with the knife before he went out where Mackenzie could see him with the binoculars. He took off his shirt and waved it just to be sure. He waited until he saw them moving out from camp, then he went back to the dead men and took their rifles and bandoliers. A good rifle, the Lebel. Maybe not as good as the new British Lee-Enfield or the new German Mauser, both with smoother bolt action, but still a well-made military rifle with a good reputation.

The civilians stared at the dead men as they filed past. Gatling walked with Mackenzie in the lead. "You say one of them yelled a lot," Mackenzie said. "Well, I didn't hear it and I have good hearing and was a lot closer than the next watcher is likely to be."

Two Marines were on either side of Frobisher, ready to grab him if he tried to make a break. Mackenzie was taking no chances; Frobisher's hands were tied. Mackenzie set a slow pace because, as he told Gatling, getting a nod of agreement, there was always the chance that they had read Urbino's signs wrong. Gatling wondered how Sarah Morrison, rich, spoiled, college-educated daughter of a Tammany chieftain, was taking it. She wanted adventure and now she was right in the thick of it, and maybe it was nothing like the thrilling stories about faraway places they published in the New York magazines. He hoped she wasn't dead.

Moving out far ahead of the others, Gatling killed the third trail-watcher at twelve noon. He knew what time it was because he looked at his watch after he wiped off the knife blade on the dead man's shirt and put it away. There was only one man, but he wasn't easy to find. Gatling finally found him lying still in thick brush and knifed him to death. Then, holding the dead man's French rifle, he waited for the others to catch up. Moving at a snail's pace, it took them an hour to do it. He had worked out the time with Mackenzie.

The third watcher had been posted three miles from the men who'd been set to watch the camp from the edge of the trees, and maybe that was how it was going to be: a watching post every three miles. He asked Frobisher how far they were from Urbino's camp, and he said he figured about ten miles. Not so bad, Gatling decided. If he had the distance right there would be two, at the most three, watching posts before they got close to Urbino's camp.

"Jesus! I don't know how you hold up under the strain," Mackenzie said. "You've already killed three watchers and you think there'll be at least two more. I wish I could help you, but I'm an ungainly kind of a man. They'd hear me coming a mile off."

Killing was thirsty work, and Gatling took a second long drink from his canteen. Mackenzie was carrying it. Getting set to kill was harder than the killing itself. All that sneaking and crawling made a man thirsty.

"You're needed where you are, Mac." Gatling took another drink. "You'll have plenty to do when it's time to move in. There's a lot of them and not enough of us, so the mortar and the light gun have to make up the difference. The French rifles ought to help, and maybe we'll get one or two more."

"Who'll be firing the Mexican rifle?"

"I'll use it as backup for the mortar, but you'll have the light gun. I've always relied on that tough little son of a bitch."

Mackenzie laughed. He worried a a lot, but he wasn't nervous. There was a difference, Gatling thought.

"You make it sound like a woman," Mackenzie said, grinning now instead of laughing.

Gatling grinned back at him. "God's truth, Mac, that little gun has proved more reliable than most women I've known."

"That's a terrible thing to say." Mackenzie hiked up his carbine sling, and had no more to say on the subject of women.

Gatling said, "Frobisher says Urbino's got Sarah tied hand and foot in his shelter, some kind of hut. That's where she was when they started out late last night. Or so he says. It's going to be tricky getting her out of there alive."

"I just thought of that a minute ago," Mackenzie said. "Oh, I realized all along, but now that we're so close—"

"We can't hold back because of Sarah." Gatling thought of

the good nights on the ship coming down from Brooklyn. "That could get her killed just as fast as doing it full force. When it comes time to hit them, then we have to hit them as hard as we can do it."

Mackenzie squinted through the sweat running into his eyes. "I hear you," he said abruptly. "Sorry, Gatling. I know you're right. The best we can do it try not to send bullets her way. Frobisher says it's the biggest shelter in camp. I'll tell the men not to shoot at it."

"Unless Urbino is in there with her."

"How the hell are we to know that?"

"You'll know if he starts shooting back at you. We have to kill him, Mac, or he'll dog us all the way to the coast. If Sarah gets killed . . . well, what is there to say?"

"Nothing," Mackenzie snapped. "That's what you can say— nothing."

The fourth trail-watcher put up a terrific fight before Gatling killed him. It had to happen: The other killings had been too easy. The watcher, sitting on a log holding his rifle, turned and grabbed Gatling's wrist as the knife flashed down. He was a squat powerful man, and he grabbed Gatling's other wrist and pulled him across the log and threw him. Gatling hit the ground hard, but came up still holding the knife and moved in fast. Instead of bolting a round, the watcher gripped the rifle by the end of the barrel and was swinging it like a club.

They circled in silence. Gatling expected the watcher to start yelling, but he didn't. Maybe he knew he was too far away to be heard. He was pretty good, the way he feinted and blocked, all the time waiting for the moment when he could crush Gatling's skull like an eggshell. He yelled when he thought he had it, and the rifle butt came swinging down. But he was a wink too late, and Gatling ducked in low and stabbed him just below the armpit, and he raised up on his toes and shuddered before he fell down and died. Gatling wiped off the knife and picked up the dead man's rifle.

"Maybe there's nobody between here and the camp,"

Mackenzie said, handing Gatling his canteen. "Frobisher thinks we can't be more than three miles out from there. Let's hope the dirty bastard is a good judge of distance."

Gatling looked at the trail, faint but clear enough to be followed, going on ahead of them. "We'll make it three miles from here to there. There has to be a cook smoke if they're anywhere close. I'll go ahead two miles, then wait for you. Give it fifteen minutes before you start out. When you get there we'll start to fan out."

Gatling had to do no more killing, at least not then. If there had been a watcher anywhere along the two miles of trail, he was gone now. That was how it was; you never could be sure about anything until it was over. He could hear Mackenzie and the others coming along the trail, but they were very close by then, and the small amount of noise they made wasn't so bad. Maybe he heard them only because he was listening so hard.

Mackenzie sent two Marines out to stand guard while the others grouped for final instructions. Gatling could see that Mackenzie wasn't too sure how well he could instruct the civilians. But they were part of the little force and he did his best. They were to fan out, and then move in slowly until they had the front of the camp covered, and part of the sides. The Marines would be spread out among them, telling them when to move, when to stand still, when to take cover.

"Don't swing the ends of the line too far around or you'll create a crossfire." Mackenzie had tied a handkerchief around his head to keep the sweat from running into his eyes. Gatling thought he looked like a long-jawed Apache with a bad sunburn. "Listen to my Marines. Do what they tell you to do. I'll be ahead of you with Gatling. Keep us in sight if possible. When you hear the mortar—that's the mortar there—that will be the signal to move in. I've told you ten times about the shelter where Miss Morrison may be. Try not to kill her, but don't hesitate because of her. Don't get killed because of her. I don't think I have to explain how she got here. But never mind. We have to get her out. Any questions?"

There were no questions.

Mackenzie said, "The mortar and the machine gun will do most of the work." He turned to Tabor, pale and sweating and sick-faced. He was leaning on a crutch made from a light tree limb. "Mr. Tabor sprained his ankle on the way here, so he will not be taking part in the attack unless he recovers between now and then. You will take your orders from my sergeant. We have two objectives: to rescue Miss Morrison and to kill Urbino. We'll have no peace as long as he's alive. You know what he looks like. Kill the bastard. Put him down in the dirt."

As Gatling picked up the mortar and the box of shells, he saw that Mackenzie had given Lebel rifles to Wheeler and Irby. Maybe they'll do all right, he thought.

They moved forward through the trees, with Gatling sweating under the weight of the mortar and the shells. Now and then he had to set down the load and rest. Maybe Sandow the Strongman could walk around with a load like that, but he was no strongman and he had to rest.

They smelled wood smoke after they'd gone about 500 yards. The smell grew stronger, and then they were close enough to hear voices. Five minutes from there they could see the wide clearing where the camp was. It was a big camp, bigger than they'd expected, and there must have been 60 or 70 men standing around or lying in the shade or doing something at the fires. Gatling moved his binoculars until he found Urbino's shelter, bigger than the others, standing at the base of a tall tree. There was no sign of Urbino.

"I see the shelter," Mackenzie said, casing his binoculars. "You want to wait a while?"

Gatling looked up through the trees. It was beginning to get dark; it would be dark in 30 minutes. It had to be now.

"Move the light gun about fifty yards forward," he told Mackenzie. "You'll have a better field of fire."

Gatling figured the elevation of the mortar while Mackenzie was getting set. Mackenzie looked back at him and waved, Gatling pushed a shell down the barrel of the mortar, and a shell went screaming into the camp. It exploded with a bright orange flash, and the ground shook and men screamed as shell fragments tore into them and huts caught fire and started to burn. Gatling lobbed shell after shell into Urbino's camp, and between the explosions he heard the light gun rattling out short bursts of bullets. It was strange to be listening to the sound of his own gun, but Mackenzie was doing it just right; a long burst, then a short burst, firing it the right way so the barrel wouldn't overheat.

Suddenly he heard Urbino's great booming voice coming through the shouts and the screams, the rattle of the light gun, the crunch of mortar. It was hard to see anything with all the fire and smoke. The huts and the brush around the camp were on fire. Gatling let loose the last shell, and then he unslung the automatic rifle and moved forward to where Mackenzie was. Mackenzie gave him a quick look, but didn't stop firing. Gatling could see better from where he was now. He used the binoculars, but failed to find Urbino. But he could hear him roaring like a madman, trying to rally his raggedy troops. Return fire had been weak, but now it started to pick up. They were finding cover and using it to shoot back, and now the bullets were coming thick and fast. Urbino kept on shouting. Gatling took a clip from his belt and pushed it into the automatic rifle, then he pulled back the activating bolt, steadied the gun, and opened fire. Behind him he heard Wheeler's people, Garth's people now, and the Marines moving up through the trees. Mackenzie turned and roared at them to take cover. "Get down! Get down! They're coming out at us!"

Some of Urbino's men had run away, but the others were trying to counterattack, driven from cover at pistol point. Urbino kept shouting, "Attack! Attack!" in Spanish. Gatling and Mackenzie fired at them as they came through the trees. The Marines and the civilians were moving forward at a crawl, hugging the ground while bullets hissed above their heads. Gatling heard a Marine voice telling them to keep their asses down. He fitted a fresh magazine into the rifle and opened up again.

Urbino's men came stumbling through the gathering dark, lead-footed and clumsy, afraid and desperately wanting not to die. Mackenzie shouted, "Open fire!" and all along the stretched-out line of Marines and civilians rifles and pistols spat fire, the French rifles making a different sound than the carbines. Gatling and Mackenzie fired steadily, killing men as the guns moved this way and that, and suddenly the counterattack fell apart and Urbino's men were running back the other way. They ran faster now; they were running for their lives.

Mackenzie gave the order to move up. Gatling pushed another magazine into the rifle. Some fire still came from the clearing. A few men were still trying to make a fight of it. Their last stand lasted no more than a few minutes; the heavy fire drove them from their position and they started to run. The light gun and the Mexican rifle brought them down. A young Marine with a dirty face shouted, "Mr. Wheeler has been killed."

One last bullet struck a tree and, except for Urbino, there was no more resistance. There was nobody left to fight: Urbino's men were dead, wounded, or had run away. Urbino was dragging Sarah Morrison from the shelter as they moved out of the trees and into the clearing. Urbino had the shiny revolver pressed to the side of her head while his left arm held her at the waist. Gatling set down the rifle and drew the Colt and started forward. Mackenzie and the others didn't move. "Get back, you," Urbino shouted. "I will kill this woman. I am telling you to go back." Gatling kept coming, thinking what difference does it make if I kill her or he does. The light wasn't so good now; the fires were burning out and there were long shadows.

Gatling got closer, but not yet close enough. "Drop that gun or I will kill her. I will do it." Urbino's voice was frantic. He's afraid, Gatling thought. He knows if he kills her he'll be dead an instant later. He can't make up his mind.

That's what he was thinking, but he knew Urbino might kill her just the same. A spasm of fear, some kind of muscular spasm, could make his finger tighten around the trigger. Something like that, Gatling thought, more accident than anything else; but it didn't matter what it was because she'd be just as dead.

He raised the long-barreled Colt and, holding the weapon at arm's length like a duelist, he aimed it at Urbino's head. Urbino ground the muzzle of the gun into Sarah Morrison's ear. He shouted, "I am taking the woman with me. Do not try to stop me or—"

Urbino didn't get to complete the threat. Gatling, with the Colt rock solid, shot him in the forehead, and he dropped like a stone.

Gatling holstered the Colt, and when he turned away from her he saw Dr. LaPlante coming toward him. The doctor, carrying his black bag, passed him without a word. Then he heard the doctor's voice and he heard her crying. She's crying now, he thought, but what will she be like a month from now? Much the same, he was fairly sure. Few people changed, not even when they wanted to.

Later, Mackenzie told him that Wheeler had been shot through the head. Gatling had nothing to say to that.

"I had one man killed, three wounded," Mackenzie said. "Garth and a surveyor named Emmerich were killed. Tabor shot Frobisher . . . shot him four times. Claimed he was trying to escape. A fine show of courage considering Frobisher's hands were tied."

"Let's get the hell out of here," Gatling said.

They buried their dead and headed for the coast.

Chapter
FOURTEEN

"It shouldn't have been handled the way it was," Gatling said. "That's all I'm saying. You don't agree?"

"Of course I agree." The colonel lay back in his big leather chair and smiled his wintry smile. "I'd be the first to agree, as you bloody well know. But this is not an ideal world, and we must take things as we find them."

They were talking about the Panama expedition. Gatling had completed his report, and it lay on Colonel Pritchett's desk. After it was edited and given to the typewriter girl, it would be sent to Hiram Maxim, in England.

"No politics, no strings. That's how an operation like that should work. Wheeler was like a one-armed juggler. Too many balls in the air and no way to catch them. He was beholden to too many people. He went to bits through every fault of his own. He was a drunk."

The colonel regarded Gatling with some amusement. "No politics, you say. That's not being realistic. Men will still be playing politics on Judgment Day. However, let's not go into that. All things considered, I'm inclined to regard the expedition as having a considerable amount of success. It has provided much useful information. It has put Panama on the map, so to speak, and there it will remain. We have the newspapers to thank for that. From now on Nicaragua will have to take a back seat. If a canal is built—and I'm quite certain it will—Panama is where they will build it.''

''The French didn't make such a good job of it.''

''The French don't have our American know-how,'' the colonel said in his brisk British accent. ''We will learn by their mistakes. Think of it, my boy. In a few years—well, let's say ten or twenty—American warships will be steaming through a magnificent canal built by and for Americans.''

The colonel was waving the flag for all it was worth. An Englishman born and bred, he didn't like the British any more because they had kicked him out of their army. He was always making nasty jokes about Queen Victoria.

''The Pacific will become the American Ocean,'' he went on. ''Our ships will be everywhere.''

''Bringing Maxim guns to Asia by the short route,'' Gatling said.

The colonel bristled. ''And what's wrong with that? Guns always go before the trader and the missionary. That's the way of history. China and all its vast wealth lies waiting. Manifest Destiny, my lad. Don't you feel a stirring in the blood?''

''If I do, it must be something I caught in Panama.''

''Such cynicism is not to your credit,'' the colonel said. The colonel was the most cynical man Gatling had ever come across. There was nothing he wouldn't do to sell guns, to make money, to advance his own position. He was greedy as well as cynical. Honest only when he had to be, he used graft and blackmail to get his way. He would start a war between Quakers and Franciscans if it put money in his pocket.

He turned a page of Gatling's report. ''I see you have good things to say about the mortar.''

''We'd all be buried in Panama if not for the mortar,'' Gatling said. ''Urbino's men were coming at us in waves. No other way we could have stopped them. The mortar killed enough of them to feed every buzzard in Central America.''

The colonel frowned. ''You killed them, not we killed them. You killed them with a weapon manufactured by the Maxim

Company. Get it right. Credit where credit is due.''

"I didn't do it for credit," Gatling told him. "Just for the money.''

"Then give credit to the weapon.''

"Kiss my weapon, Colonel.''

"Very droll, I'm sure." The colonel ran his finger down the page. "You have reservations about the Mondragon automatic rifle?''

Gatling liked the Mondragon well enough. A well-made and dependable weapon, but only if used under the right conditions. Dust—and especially mud—were its worst enemies. It needed better seals. It needed a shorter barrel. Colonel Mondragon was on to something good, but his automatic rifle needed more work before it became a standard infantry weapon.

Gatling told all that to the colonel, although there was no need. It was all in the report.

"I'm sure Mr. Maxim will set it right," the colonel said, disappointed that the Mondragon hadn't worked out as well as he'd expected. His agents had stolen the new Mexican rifle, but the way his mind worked, it now belonged to the Maxim Company.

Another page was turned. "You have no complaints about the Maximite. I didn't think you would. You'll be interested to know that while you were in Panama Mr. Maxim wrote and informed me that the company expects to develop an even more powerful explosive.''

"That's great," Gatling said. Someday Maxim and his brother were going to blow up the world. Or the Du Ponts were. Somebody was. But, for better or worse, the weapons business was his business, and he had no special feelings about it. No, that wasn't true: He loved his bloody trade.

"You have something to add that isn't in here?" the colonel wanted to know. "You know I'm always interested in what you have to say." Gatling got a smile with all the warmth of a mortuary slab. "At least when it comes to weapons.''

The colonel was always trying to get something for nothing. Any ideas Gatling had, if they were usable, he would claim as his own. Not that Gatling gave a damn: He tested weapons, he didn't make them.

"The military could use a short bolt-action rifle for jungle fighting," he said. "Light and short. Maybe a rubber butt to cut down weight. The Springfield carbine isn't bad, but it loads one round at a time, and the hammer sticks out too much. Tends to snag on things."

The colonel twirled the ends of his mustache. "Don't mean to be a wet blanket, old man, but not much fighting's done in the jungles. But please continue."

"Jungle fighting is always done in the dark," Gatling said. "Black dark at night, half dark by day. The trees block any light there is. A man fires a rifle in there, the flash gives him away."

"So this rifle needs a flash-concealer, a flash-hider." Colonel Pritchett looked pleased with himself. "That shouldn't be too much of a problem. Something to diffuse the flash, that is. Mr. Maxim . . ."

The telephone bolted to the wall behind the colonel's desk rang furiously, and he got up to answer it. "Yes," he said cautiously. "This is Pritchett here. Oh, your boat has just docked, has it? Yes, I'll be there. Goodbye."

"I'm afraid I have to go out," he told Gatling. "We'll discuss this new rifle idea some other time. By the way, I almost forgot. Miss Morrison of the *New York World* telephoned you this morning. She would like you to ring her back. The number is seven-two-five. Got it?"

"Seven-two-five," Gatling repeated.

"Miss Morrison sounds like a right corker," the colonel said. "Good-looking, eh? I thought as much. And rich to boot. You sly old dog."

"You think I'm after this woman for her money?"

"It's one way to get it."

"I don't care how much money she has. She broke my balls in Panama."

"Indeed she did, Gatling," the colonel said, though he knew nothing about it. "And she'll break them here in New York.

Take it from me, dear friend, you're not the marrying kind. Is anybody? Married life is dreadful. There's absolutely nothing to be said for it. It's a life sentence with no possibility of parole. A man may escape, perhaps, but he is never paroled. I can hear her even now: 'Gatling dear, you've been getting gun grease on the new carpet, you naughty boy.' Or even worse: 'Mother is becoming terribly suspicious about those long business trips you take. You go away for months, as if you've been wasting your essences in the company of fallen women.''

Gatling said, ''All right, Colonel. Enough stale jokes for one day.''

Colonel Pritchett raised his bird's-nest eyebrows. ''Oh, I wasn't joking, my boy. Come to think of it, though, matrimony is a joke. It's a music-hall act where the husband is the one who gets slapped by the pig's bladder. Why is the husband always the butt of every matrimonial joke since time began?''

''Why is he, Mister Bones?''

''It's because he himself is a joke, a buffoon, an object of ridicule. Actually, he is more to be pitied than scorned. My dear boy, I know whereof I speak.''

''You were married at one time,'' Gatling reminded the bitter old Englishman. ''Was it as bad as all that?''

''Haw!'' That was how the colonel laughed. ''Bad? Why do you think I spent so many years in India? Because I liked the bloody place? I should think not. My sole reason for remaining there so long was to avoid being shackled by the monstrous chains of marital bliss. Don't do it, I beg you. Run . . . run as if Cerberus itself were after you.''

''What's a Cerberus, Colonel?''

''A three-headed dog in classical mythology.''

''Miss Morrison is no dog,'' Gatling said. ''Mind telling me what all this bullshit is about? If I do decide to telephone her, probably all we'll do is have lunch at Rector's and visit the Metropolitan Museum. What could be more innocent than that?''

The colonel sighed. ''Ah, yes, these things usually have an innocent beginning.''

The plans Gatling had for Sarah Morrison, if he called her, were along entirely different lines.

"Rector's! Since when have you been going to Rector's? Stay away from the place. It's too expensive for a miser like you. Yes. Yes. I know. Your Zuni philanthropy."

Gatling looked hard at the crafty Britisher. "You're just afraid I'll quit the company and you'll have nobody to test your weapons. That's the straight of it, isn't it? That's what's behind all this downgrading of marriage."

The colonel gave Gatling his glacial smile. "Well, yes, there is that consideration. I feel for you as if you were my own son. It would cause me great distress if you were to become entrapped in this female's web. The female of the species, etcetera. As Mr. Kipling wrote so succinctly."

Gatling picked up his hat off the floor. "I'd probably write like that if I had a wife that looked like that. I've seen newspaper photographs."

"Now there's a real Cerberus," the colonel said. "All I can say to you is, watch your step. As some saint or other said, 'The road to Hell is paved with good intentions.' And now I must see a man about a dogma. Haw! Jolly good, eh? In point of fact, he's a Peruvian priest who wants to start a revolution. I'd like to give you this very profound thought before you leave. There's no earthly reason why you should climb up on the cross with the rest of the martyrs. God bless you, my boy."

Going down the stairs to the street, Gatling wondered if the colonel might not be right about Sarah Morrison—not that the old bastard knew a damned thing about her. Out in the street, looking for a hansom cab, he still hadn't made up his mind. If he did call her, what happened after that would be like going over Niagara Falls without the barrel. But if he didn't call her, he might be sorry he hadn't.

He took a quarter from his pocket and flipped it in the air.

SPECIAL OFFER! SAVE $5.00!

Talk is cheap — bullets are cheaper.
That's...

PREACHER'S LAW

In the aftermath of the civil war, Jeremy Preacher rode home to find his plantation burned to the ground, his parents slaughtered and his sister brutally raped and murdered. Blood would flow, men would die, and Preacher would be avenged — no matter how long it took. Join Preacher's bloody crusade for justice — from 1865 to 1908.

____2741-0 #7: **RAIDERS**
by Barry Myers $2.75US/$3.75CAN

____2715-1 #6: **REBEL**
by Barry Myers $2.75US/$3.75CAN

____2588-4 #5: **SLAUGHTER AT TEN SLEEP**
by Dean L. McElwain $2.75US/$3.75CAN

____2576-0 #4: **THE LAST GUNFIGHT**
by Dean L. McElwain $2.75US/$3.75CAN

____2552-3 #3: **THE GAVEL AND THE GUN**
by Dean L. McElwain $2.75US/$3.75CAN

____2528-0 #2: **TRAIL OF DEATH**
by Dean L. McElwain $2.75US/$3.75CAN

____2508-6 #1: **WIDOW MAKER**
by Dean L. McElwain $2.75US/$3.75CAN

Don't miss out on this special offer!
Order all seven books and pay only *$17.50* total! NO postage and handling charge! You save almost $5.00!

LEISURE BOOKS
ATTN: Customer Service Dept.
276 5th Avenue, New York, NY 10001

Please send me the book(s) checked above. I have enclosed $ _____
Add $1.25 for shipping and handling for the first book; $ .30 for each book thereafter. No cash, stamps, or C.O.D.s. All orders shipped within 6 weeks. Canadian orders please add $1.00 extra postage.

Name _____

Address _____

City _____ State _____ Zip _____
Canadian orders must be paid in U.S. dollars payable through a New York banking facility. ☐ Please send a free catalogue.

BUCKSKIN

The hard-riding, hard-bitten Adult Western series that's hotter'n a blazing pistol and as tough as the men who tamed the frontier.

#18: REMINGTON RIDGE   by Kit Dalton
____2509-4 $2.95US/$3.95CAN

#17: GUNSMOKE GORGE   by Kit Dalton
____2484-5 $2.50US/$3.25CAN

#16: WINCHESTER VALLEY   by Kit Dalton
____2463-2 $2.50US/$3.25CAN

#15: SCATTERGUN   by Kit Dalton
____2439-X $2.50US/$3.25CAN

#10: BOLT ACTION   by Roy LeBeau
____2315-6 $2.50US/$2.95CAN

#5: GUNSIGHT GAP   by Roy LeBeau
____2189-7 $2.75US/$2.95CAN

LEISURE BOOKS
ATTN: Customer Service Dept.
276 5th Avenue, New York, NY 10001

Please send me the book(s) checked above. I have enclosed $ _____
Add $1.25 for shipping and handling for the first book; $ .30 for each book thereafter. No cash, stamps, or C.O.D.s. All orders shipped within 6 weeks. Canadian orders please add $1.00 extra postage.

Name _____

Address _____

City _____ State _____ Zip _____
Canadian orders must be paid in U.S. dollars payable through a New York banking facility.   ☐ Please send a free catalogue.